ellen potter

SCHOLASTIC INC.
New York Toronto London Auckland
Sydney Mexico City New Delhi Hong Kong

ISBN 978-0-545-28673-2

12 11 10 9 8 7 6 5 4 3   11 12 13 14 15/0

Printed in the U.S.A.   40

First Scholastic printing, September 2010

Design by Marikka Tamura

For Will Rabinovich

Acknowledgments

I'm not nearly as smart as Owen Birnbaum, so I needed a lot of help to write this book. I am lucky enough, however, to know several *very* smart people. Special thanks to Will Rabinovich, who patiently explained electromagnetic radiation and dwarf stars and helped me work out a clever scenario for Owen's Nemesis invention. Special thanks also to my husband, Adam, who has been dissecting electronic devices since he was a boy genius and understands how things work better than anyone I know.

While I was researching this book, I was lucky enough to connect with the wonderful Jim Sky, editor for *Radio-Sky Journal,* http://radiosky.com. He generously gave me a crash course on radio telescopes as well as some unusually creative ideas as to how a twelve-year-old boy might be able to pick up signals from a star. I can't thank you enough, Jim! For anybody who is interested in trying to build their own simple radio telescope and observe Jupiter, the sun, and the galactic background, Jim suggests peeking at the Radio Jove Project, from NASA, http://radiojove.gsfc.nasa.gov/.

Many thanks to Urgyen Khetsatsang for all his help regarding Tibetan customs. Thanks to Jason and Tyler Ward, my kid informants, and to Adam, Valerie Akers, Stella and Koen Boyer, Jessica Dougherty, and Bill and Sharon Morrow for giving me the gift of time to write this book. Thanks to Ian, who has been patiently waiting for "his book" to be finished so that he can build a garage for his toy cars out of my author copies.

As always, a galaxyful of gratitude to two superstars, my agent, Alice Tasman, and my editor, Michael Green!

1

My name is Owen Birnbaum, and I'm probably fatter than you are. This isn't my low self-esteem talking. This is pure statistics. I'm five foot two and I weigh 156 pounds. That's 57 percent fatter than the national average for a twelve-year-old boy.

I'm also probably smarter than you. I don't mean that as an insult. Again, statistics. They had my IQ tested in the second grade. I won't tell you my score. Actually, I *can't* tell you my score because I promised my mother I wouldn't do that anymore. I used to tell everyone. My mother said that was obnoxious. I think she was also worried about giving my sister, Jeremy, a complex. Jeremy is a year younger than I am and not the brightest crayon in the box. She's a good kid. Just very so-so in the cerebral cortex region.

I'm sure you've noticed that a lot of books start out with some kid's first day at a new school. You can see why, of course. It makes for great suspense. The new kid is feeling very nervous. Everything seems slightly sinister. Half the kids in the class look like they want to smash his face in, and the other half look like they would love to see the first half of the class smash his face in.

The thing is, when you are fatter and smarter than the national average, practically every day is like the first day at a new school.

So, I'm starting this book on a Tuesday, and school has already been in session for a few weeks now. I go to Martha Doxie School in New York City. A three-story redbrick nightmare of educational progress. They have this thing called "The Deskless Classroom," where everyone does what interests them. We have different workstations . . . science, writing, global studies. We choose what we want to study at any given time. No desks. Just workstations. Which are basically desks.

The school's motto is Compassion, Not Competition.

The thing is, most kids don't give a flea's fart about compassion.

Exhibit A: My missing Oreo cookies.

Kids who bring their own lunches put them up on the top shelf of a hallway closet just outside their classrooms. Mom always puts my lunch in a cloth sack, which is made of recycled socks or something like that. My name is printed on it very clearly. She always puts three Oreos in an eco-container, which is made of recycled shower curtains (I'm not kidding, they really are made from shower curtains). Three Oreos at lunch. That's our agreement, since I started this new diet. At first, she tried to give me some of the fake Oreos, with the organic ingredients and stuff like barley and cane juice, but I put my foot down there. The cookie part actually tasted pretty close to the original, but the cream inside was all wrong. When you opened the cookie and tried to scrape the cream off with your teeth, it all came off in one sticky disk and sort of dangled from the inside of your top teeth. If you didn't catch it in time, it just plopped down into your lap. Completely unacceptable.

We argued about this for a long time, but I wouldn't budge on the issue, so she finally gave in. I've had three bona fide Oreos in my lunch ever since. It's a ritual for me. I look forward to them. I really do. It's like a spiritual thing. No matter how lousy my morning was, those three Oreo cookies remind me that life also has its high points. Its moments of bliss.

If there was any day I needed a moment of bliss, it was that day.

The Martha Doxie School is progressive in everything except gym class. As far as gym goes, they are totally conventional. Bad uniforms. Ridiculous stretching exercises that make your bad uniform ride up into all the wrong nooks and crannies. Ropes to burn your inner thighs on, volleyballs to slam at each other's heads, basketballs to pass only to your friends. In gym class the school's motto reverses itself.

Competition, Not Compassion.

The gym teacher is Mr. Wooly. A nice, cozy, snuggly

name. I really think that people should be named more appropriately. They used to do that back in the fourteenth century. If you were a potter in the fourteenth century, you were named Mr. Potter. If you father made beer, you were Mr. Brewer. No surprises.

Back in the fourteenth century, Mr. Wooly would have been named Mr. A Few Fries Short of a Happy Meal.

Mr. Walks like a Constipated Ape.

Mr. Hates Unathletic Kids and Enjoys Seeing Them Suffer.

In the locker room, I tinkered around with my combination lock for a while, waiting until most of the boys were changed and heading out to the gym. I always do that. When the locker room was pretty much empty, I quickly changed into the gym uniform of white T-shirt and blue shorts. I do it at lightning speed in order to make it out to the gym on time. It takes thirty-four seconds on a good day. Forty-six seconds if I have to undo any buttons. Then I rushed out onto the gym floor. Someone made a fart sound as I passed. That happens quite a bit, actually.

Mr. Wooly was up front, engrossed in moving odd-looking equipment out of the supply room. I took my assigned spot on the 12D grid—the numbers run along the front and back walls of the gym and the letters run along the side walls of the gym. I stood right next to Andre Bertoni. He was already stretching, even though he didn't have to yet. He swung his adult-sized muscle-bound arms from side to side and bounced on his toes, as though he was preparing for the Olympic 400-meter dash.

"What's up, Flapjack?" he asked, flashing me one of his movie star smiles. He's called me Flapjack for the past two years. I don't know why. It's idiotic, but people have called me worse.

"What do you think all that stuff is for?" I asked him nervously, looking at the equipment that Mr. Wooly was arranging. There were stands with metal poles across them, beefy-looking, vinyl-covered gizmos, loads of floor mats.

"Looks like we'll be doing some gymnastics," Andre said breezily.

"Oh, crap." I said it under my breath, but Andre heard.

"Hey, Flapjack," Andre hissed, tipping his head in a gesture for me to come closer to him. I glanced over at Mr. Wooly. He was kneeling down, unrolling a long blue mat on the floor.

"Yeah?" I said, moving closer a little cagily. You never know with Andre.

"Why don't you just get one of those fat exemptions?" Andre said quietly.

"What?" I felt my shoulders stiffen up.

"A fat exemption. You know. Your doctor writes it for you. It says you don't have to do gym because you're so fat that exercise could make your heart stop." He thumped me on the back. He thumps me a lot.

I grunted and started to walk back to my spot, but

Andre grabbed my arm. "No joke, Flapjack. Look at that stuff." He nodded toward the apparatus. "You'll cripple yourself! And Wooly will love it. It's not worth the pain."

That's the thing about Andre Bertoni. I can never tell if he's being nice or mean. I often think I should hate him, but somehow he makes it difficult.

"Whenever Mr. Birnbaum is finished flirting with Mr. Bertoni, we can get started on our stretches!" Mr. Wooly had finished unrolling the mat and was now glaring at me with his ape arms crossed over his ape chest. A chorus of snickers and catcalls rose up from the class.

I have *no* trouble hating Mr. Wooly, incidentally.

Mr. Wooly led us through a bunch of ridiculous stretching exercises. He didn't do them himself. He never does. He just barks out instructions. That day I didn't mind doing the stretching, though. It delayed what was to come. My eyes kept drifting over to the apparatus next to Mr. Wooly. It looked evil. It looked like it was specially designed to humiliate me.

I actually started to consider the fat exemption. I wondered if that was a real possibility. Mom had taken me in for a checkup before school, and the doctor had clucked his tongue as he read the scale. Then he gave Mom what they call a "firm talking to." I felt really bad for her. It's not her fault, after all.

That doctor might give me a fat exemption.

But I couldn't do that. I have too much pride.

There's that saying, "Pride cometh before the fall."

Yeah, I thought as I looked at the gymnastic equipment, there was going to be a lot of falling involved.

"All right, ladies and gentlemen!" Mr. Wooly clapped so loudly that it echoed throughout the gym.

PS, this is an all-boy class. No ladies. Hardy har har.

"For the next three weeks we are going to try something different. We are going to challenge our bodies. We are going to test our fears."

Andre Bertoni caught my eye and winked. I have no idea why. Maybe he was relishing the thought of having his fears tested. Or watching my fears being tested.

I don't think I was the only one who was nervous about this gymnastic stuff, though. I had enough presence of mind to look around at the faces of the other boys. A lot of them were eying the gymnastic apparatus apprehensively. One really skinny kid named Justin Esposito was actually clutching at his stomach as though he were going to be sick. I felt so bad for him that I almost forgot to feel bad for me. Nima would have liked that. He would have thought it was very Buddhist of me.

I'll tell you more about Nima later.

Mr. Wooly explained about all the apparatus and what we were going to be doing on each one in the next few weeks, whether we liked it or not. We'd be flipping and flying in the air. We'd regularly be defying the law of gravity. But first . . . He paused and looked around at all our faces. We stared back at him, waiting. He loved it, you could tell.

"First, we are going to learn how to do a somersault properly."

A lot of the boys groaned, including Andre. I, on the other hand, felt like I had been handed a death sentence reprieve from the governor. Justin Esposito actually smiled.

Big mistake.

"We'll start with Mr. Esposito, since he is so overjoyed at the thought of doing somersaults. Gather around the mat, gentleworms." Hardy har har.

We stood on either side of the long blue mat, while Mr. Wooly guided Justin Esposito to the front of it. Poor Justin looked like he was about to vomit. I was actually wishing that he *would* vomit so he'd be spared. A vomit exemption. But seeing someone vomit makes me want to vomit, so I took back the wish. I didn't think I'd tell Nima about that, since it was less than empathetic.

"Get down on all fours, Mr. Esposito," Mr. Wooly commanded.

Justin did. "Now put your head down two inches in front of the line of your shoulders," Mr. Wooly said. "Legs hip width apart, toes tucked under, tailbone down."

Justin Esposito's ears were turning crimson, and he looked like he was in pain.

"Push your left hip out a little. Now tuck your head down and push with your toes. Now! Push! Now!"

Justin's right leg kicked up and he toppled over to his right side. People laughed. I did too. I'm not proud of it. I almost didn't tell you. I definitely will never tell Nima.

Mr. Wooly could not have been more pleased. He didn't even have Justin try again. It would have ruined the moment if he'd actually managed to do a somersault on the second try.

The next boy up managed a decent somersault. The one after that did too. But then came a kid who was one of the lousier basketball players, and he failed miserably. What I noticed, though, was that when the athletic boys were on the mat, Mr. Wooly hardly gave them any instruction at all. However, when one of us nonathletic types came to the mat, Mr. Wooly would bark out all these instructions about where to put their head and how to adjust their hips, and by the time the kid was all situated he looked as stiff and unnatural as if he were playing a game of Twister. When he pushed off into a tumble, he'd fall in this cockeyed way, which would make everyone laugh. Except for me. I wasn't laughing any more. It was becoming clear to me that Mr. Wooly was setting these kids up. The way he had them place their bodies, they were bound to fall in some weird way. It was pure physics.

It made me so mad I wanted to rat on Mr. Wooly. I didn't, though. I'm very nonconfrontational. But I wouldn't laugh anymore.

"And next comes Mr. Birnbaum! Show us how it's done, Mr. Birnbaum." Mr. Wooly was already snickering. A pre-guffaw snicker. He was really looking forward to this. The fattest kid in class, flopping on the mat like a giant ravioli. Hysterical.

I walked up to the edge of the mat, avoiding the faces of my classmates. I could hear them laughing already.

"This is going to be so excellent," I heard someone say.

"All right, Birnbaum, down on all fours." Mr. Wooly started yelling his instructions at me. "Arms shoulders' width apart. Head tucked. Rump to the sky. The birds will think the moon has fallen." Everyone laughed at this. He waited till the laughter died down. "Okay. Now push your right hip out slightly."

That was it. Wooly's little trick to get me to fall funny.

"Come on, Birnbaum. Push out your right hip," he said.

I wouldn't do it. And you know what? It was less about not wanting to fall funny than it was about Mr. Wooly thinking he was smarter than I was. He really thought no one knew what he was up to. That just deep-fried me.

"If I push out my right hip," I said, my voice sounding strangled because of the odd angle of my head, "I'll topple to the side when I tumble."

"Don't whine," Mr. Wooly snarled. "Just do what I tell you to do, Birnbaum. There are other people waiting their turn. Now, push out your right hip and shove off from your toes."

"It won't work that way. It can't. It's obvious. I mean, it's just simple physics."

I probably shouldn't have said that. Mr. Wooly is pretty

stupid. You should never let stupid people know that *you* know they're stupid. Particularly when they are your gym teacher.

Mr. Wooly went very quiet then. My head was still tucked under my chin, so I couldn't see Mr. Wooly's face, but I could see the faces of some of my classmates. They were looking in the direction of Mr. Wooly, their eyes wide. I started to get scared. Untucking my chin, I rolled back on the balls of my feet.

"Freeze, Birnbaum," Mr. Wooly said.

I froze. I was in roughly the position of a frog about to leap.

"Stay . . . right . . . there." He wasn't shouting now. He sounded, in fact, like he had an idea. I was close to terrified.

I heard his sneakers squeaking against the polished gym floor as he walked away. Then I heard the squeal of the equipment door opening. There was some murmuring among the class as everyone wondered what on earth he was doing.

"Hang in there, Flapjack," I heard Andre say.

You see what I mean about him?

My thighs were beginning to burn from holding the awkward position. I didn't move, though. I heard the sound of clanking in the equipment room, as though Mr. Wooly was rummaging around for something. How bad could it be? I reasoned. He can't really do anything to physically hurt me. He'd get in too much trouble for that. And there were witnesses.

But then I remembered that Mr. Wooly was a few fries short of a Happy Meal. That was when my heart started pounding so hard I thought it might stop.

2

The thing that he brought out of the equipment closet had buckles and straps and some nasty-looking hardware. I couldn't tell what it was exactly, though, because I was staring at it between my knees, upside-down. Also, it was all jumbled up in Mr. Wooly's ape hands and parts of it were dragging on the floor.

Not good, I thought.

Someone said a word that I won't repeat, except to say that it had an "Oh" before it and an exclamation point after it. Mr. Wooly didn't even bother to yell at the kid for saying it. In fact, he smiled a little bit as if to say, "You got that right, pal."

"Keep still, Mr. Birnbaum. This will only take a minute," Wooly said. Suddenly, I was tangled in a web of heavy straps and Mr. Wooly was clacking buckles and clicking hooks. When it stopped there were a few seconds of dead silence. Then the snickering began.

"Woof," someone said.

It took me a moment to realize what had happened. I saw Mr. Wooly step in front of me and then back up. He was holding a long strap. He gave it a quick yank, and I felt a tug from the straps that were secured around my torso. He had put me in a halter, like a dog, and he was holding my leash.

"Okay, Birnbaum. Since you can't manage to do a simple somersault on your own, I'll have to help you do one."

For the next ten minutes I was yanked across the mat and forced to flop around in the most degrading way. I caught fleeting glimpses of my classmates' faces as I tumbled around. Most of them were pink with hysteria. And of course there were the comments. They didn't even bother to lower their voices, knowing instinctively that Mr. Wooly wouldn't care.

"Time to cut back on the puppy chow, Owen!"

"That's the fattest poodle I've ever seen!"

And so on.

It was Justin Esposito who bothered me the most. His hand was pressed against his mouth and his eyes were wide. It was exactly like one of those faces you see in the horror movies, where the Boy Scout wakes up to see a man with no nose and ten-inch iron claws tearing a hole in his pup tent. I was that vision of horror for Justin Esposito. That's how bad it all looked.

My friend Nima told me about these Tibetan monks who built a stone wall on a cliff by levitating huge rocks eight hundred feet into the air. During moments like these

I sort of lift out of my body, rising up out of the situation, like a levitating rock. I'm there but I'm not there. It's my way of dealing. But Justin's face was holding me down, making me feel the full awfulness of what was happening.

"There now." Mr. Wooly dropped the leash suddenly. "I think that helped you get the hang of things."

He had a funny look on his face, as though he had suddenly become a little scared about what he'd just done.

"Unbuckle him, Mr. Esposito!" Mr. Wooly ordered angrily, like the harness had been Justin's idea.

Justin rushed over and fumbled with the hooks while I sat back on my haunches, my face burning, my eyes focused on an indent on the mat where my head had been. It was slowly filling out, erasing what had just happened. When Justin undid the final buckle, he jumped up and away from me. The other kids were looking at me kind of funny too. They seemed nervous, like Mr. Wooly. I think they expected me to snap. It was a strange sensation. For a moment I felt really powerful. I felt large, but not in a fat way.

The spotlight was on me. I smiled. First at all the kids and then at Mr. Wooly. They didn't know what to do. They all stared at their sneakers in shame, including Mr. Wooly.

That's not true. That's not what I did. That's what Nima would have done. Here's what I did:

1. Turned red as shrimp cocktail sauce
2. Lost control of all the muscles in my face
3. Cried

4. No, sobbed
5. No, bawled like a three-year-old in Wal-Mart

Mr. Wooly looked scared and also disgusted. Most of the other kids just looked disgusted. I had the opportunity to snap, to have a volcanic eruption of pure outrage, but I had botched it. Mr. Wooly told me to go to the locker room and collect myself. As I passed Andre, he slapped the back of my neck. I think it was meant to be reassuring, but then again he may just have taken the opportunity to slap me.

By the time lunch rolled around, I had collected myself, though my eyes were still swollen. I looked around the lunchroom for Izzy Shank, the kid I always sit with. He wasn't at our usual table. It didn't take a genius to see why. Mason Ragg was sitting there, all by himself, of course, since no one else would dare sit near him. More about Mason Ragg later.

When I sat down by Izzy, he looked at me carefully, noting the swollen eyes, I'm sure. He didn't ask me about it, though. That's one reason I like Izzy. He doesn't make a big deal about things. He's the least dramatic person I know.

I opened my lunch sack and pulled out my shredded-tofu sandwich (there's not enough mayo in New York City to make that taste better than it sounds) and my bottle of pomegranate green tea. That was when I noticed that the recycled shower curtain eco-container was empty. It was even sealed back up, and those recycled containers are tricky to seal. They don't snap closed nice and easy like Tupperware. You really have to work at it.

Anyway, the Oreos were gone. I stared and stared into the empty, sealed container and shook the sad black crumbs that were lying on the bottom. I couldn't believe it.

"I can't believe it!" I said.

"What?" Izzy asked. Izzy's voice is as deep as a forty-year-old man's talking into a bullhorn, by the way. I think it's because of some glandular condition. I forgot what it's called, but basically he's huge. Six foot five, and still growing.

"Someone stole my Oreos!" I shoved the empty container at him and he took it in his hands, which happen to be the size of Jeremy's whole face. He gazed into the cloudy-looking container like he was staring into a crystal ball. In a way he was. My future lay in that empty container.

"They sealed the container back up," he said.

"I know!" I was momentarily pleased that Izzy had noticed too. That little fact had struck me as totally perverse. Who is so cool and collected while stealing that they take the time to seal a difficult-to-seal eco-container back up?

I looked around the lunchroom. Everyone looked suspicious but no one was eating any Oreos as far as I could see. I watched carefully all through lunch. Izzy did too. Nothing.

"Check teeth!" I hissed at him.

We paced through the lunchroom, trying to look inconspicuous as we searched for someone with black stuff caught between their teeth. Honestly, I don't know what we would have done if we found someone who did. It would be hard to prove that it came from Oreos rather than a Ho Ho or something like that. Besides which, neither Izzy nor I are what you would call confrontational. Yes, Izzy is the biggest person in the school, but he's more of a pacifist than I am. And I'm only a pacifist because I'm terrified of getting hurt. My sister, Jeremy, on the other hand, is always happy to pummel someone, especially if it's on my behalf. But Jeremy's grade has lunch before ours, so she wasn't around.

My eyes fell on Mason Ragg, who was sitting at our usual table. He was placed in my class a week and half ago. He'd been transferred from one of the other public schools. The word around school was that he'd been transferred because he was "unmanageable." That was another thing about the Martha Doxie School—they prided themselves in enrolling kids who didn't fit in at mainstream schools, including bona fide psychopaths, like Mason Ragg. People said that he carried a switchblade knife in his sock. They said in his last school, he had tried to strangle one of the girls in his class with her Molly Wildchild necklace (you've probably seen the commercials for the junk, but if you haven't, it's this lavender-haired cartoon character that girls just go insane over. Not Jeremy, though, of course). The girl's older brother threw an M-80 firecracker at Mason's face in retaliation. That was the story that went around school anyway. It was certainly possible. One whole side of his face was badly scarred. The skin was all bumpy and puckered, twisting up the right side of his lips so that he looked like he was always sneering. He resembled an evil character out of a comic book, no kidding, and he always looked like he was trying to catch someone staring at him.

Now he had.

You know why?

Because sitting on the table in front of him, stacked in a tidy little column, were three Oreo cookies.

"What are you staring at?" he asked in a quiet voice.

"Cool scar," I said. I really did. I do stuff like that when I'm nervous and can't think of what to say.

I can't repeat his response, though. Use your imagination, you won't be wrong.

"Sorry," I said.

That's correct, you heard me. I said sorry to the kid who stole my moment of bliss.

You might have too. Did I mention that Mason Ragg's right eye is a spooky milky blue while his left one is brown?

"Too bad about the cookies, man," Izzy said after the period buzzer sounded and we had to go our separate ways. "But no use tangling with Ragg. He has a buck knife strapped to his arm."

"I heard it was a switchblade in his sock," I said.

"Does it matter? I mean, really?"

"No."

"Hey. Keep the faith." Izzy could say things like that, which might sound sort of cool if a non-giant said them. But when he said them, it sounded like one of those deep, garbled voices you hear on the subway speaker system. You know, "Ninety-sixth Street and Broadway. Watch the closing doors. Keep the faith."

"Thanks, Izzy."

He squeezed my shoulder. It hurt. I didn't say "Ow," though, because he was only trying to be nice, and he couldn't help being insanely strong.

3

After school I waited for Jeremy and we walked home together, like we always do. I was in a lousy mood, but she was in a very good one. Suspiciously good. She strode along beside me with a small, secretive smile.

"What?" I said.

"Nothing. Just a gwab thing, that's all."

"By the way, I think there's a girl in my class who's a gwab," I said.

"Who? Oh, Rachel somebody or other, you mean?" Jeremy said.

"Rachel Lowry."

"Nah. She looks like a gwab, but she's not. Anyway, all the gwabs are in sixth grade not seventh. Hey, do people ever get expelled from our school?"

"Why?" I looked at her. She was still smiling a small, secretive smile. I didn't like it. "What did you do? Is it something about gwab?"

It's not "gwab," actually, but GWAB. Girls Who Are

Boys. Jeremy joined the club two weeks ago. There are seven other girls in the club and they have all changed their names to boys' names. They only wear boys' clothes and cut their hair in boy haircuts. Jeremy didn't cut her hair. I don't know how she got away with it, since GWAB is pretty strict. Jeremy is stubborn, though. Her hair is bright red, straight as a ruler, and reaches the last vertebra in her spine. Jeremy used to hate it when she was younger because someone in her class told her that redheads were freaks of nature. But our mother told her that redheads were genetically more courageous than other people and that she should always wear her hair long, like a warrior's badge of honor. I don't think there is any biological accuracy to that statement, by the way. In any case, Jeremy never cut her hair, except for a trim at the barbershop every now and then.

"We all signed our boy names on our math test," she said.

"But how will Mr. Shackly know who you are?"

"He won't. He'll have to ask. Then we will stand up in class and publicly declare that we are to be called by our boy names from now on."

"He won't do it, you know," I said. Mr. Shackly is one of the tougher teachers at our school.

"He'll have to," Jeremy said simply. "We won't answer him if he calls us by our girl names."

I groaned. There was going to be trouble. The GWAB members were pretty intense. I've seen them around, looking very determined. They recruited Jeremy after they saw her get into a fight with a boy in her class. They said she had the right stuff, and she agreed to join. I don't think she did it because she actually wants to be a boy. I think she did it because she was just lonely. Things have been a little topsy-turvy for us these past two years—new school, new apartment. New life. I think Jeremy was just glad to have some friends again. Plus, she loves a good fight and so do most of the GWAB members. It was a perfect fit, really.

"Hey! Flapjack!"

Jeremy and I both turned around to see Andre Bertoni jogging up to us. We occasionally meet him as we're walking to or from school since he lives right across the street from us, in this fancy apartment building called Fuji Towers.

More about Fuji Towers later.

Andre was wearing his big-screen smile. I heard Jeremy swallow hard. Really, I heard it. She has a huge crush on Andre. She's a sensible kid in every other way.

"How you doing, man?" Andre said when he caught up to us. "Hey, Caitlin."

"She's not Caitlin anymore," I told him. "She's changed her name to Jeremy."

"But that's a boy's name," he said, his smile now looking confused.

"That's right," I said.

He looked over at Jeremy, and her face became roughly the same color as her hair.

"You know what I would do if I were you, Flapjack?" he said, looking away from Jeremy.

Kill yourself? I thought. But I said. "I have no idea, Andre."

"I'd sue," he said confidently.

"Sue who?" I asked.

"The school," Andre said. "Because of what Mr. Wooly did to you."

"What did he do?" Jeremy's ears pricked up at this. She was always looking out for unfair things that people had done to other people, especially if it involved me.

"Nothing, nothing," I said.

"What did he do to Owen?" she addressed this to Andre, completely forgetting herself and yanking Andre's jacket sleeve. Andre looked a bit surprised himself. He smoothed down the material of his jacket (it was probably some fancy European jacket that his father had brought back from some super-suave country).

"He put him in a dog harness and forced him to roll around on the floor," Andre said.

"It was nothing," I insisted.

Jeremy's mouth gawped open. For a moment I thought she was about to bellow. She's a little bit like a superhero with no superhero talents. She despises bullies and loves underdogs, much like the classic superhero. But she's thin as a coat hanger and on the shortish side, and all she can do is punch reasonably hard with her bony knuckles. No jet-propelled flying, no invisibility skills.

"I'll pulverize him," she said in this quiet voice. It was impressive. Even Andre gave her his full attention for about seven seconds before he turned back to me.

"Tell your mother to call my dad. He might even be willing to take the case himself." Then he jogged on, leaving me with the dismal, fleeting image of Mom sitting in Mr. Bertoni's cushy leather office chair (it had to be leather) discussing how I had been trussed up in a dog harness.

"How could Wooly treat you like that!" Jeremy blurted. *"You!"*

She has this idea about me. She thinks I am a better person than I actually am. Nicer, funnier, smarter. I mean, I am smart, but she thinks I'm a genius, which I am not. Not quite. I missed genius rank by one point.

What she didn't know was that people were always treating me like Mr. Wooly had, or thereabouts. I mean, I do think she understood I wasn't exactly popular, but sixth graders and seventh graders live in totally different universes. She didn't know that I had become an official bully magnet, the punch line of every joke. That people made fart noises when I walked by and murmured things like "Fatty Fatty Ding Dong." She didn't know and I wanted to keep it that way.

"Just forget it," I said. "It was no big deal."

But the anger was leaving her face and being replaced by a look of despair. "Oh, Owen. What a world."

They were gut-squeezing words. It made me think of other stuff besides Mr. Wooly and stolen Oreo cookies. I

25

glanced at Jeremy. She was frowning down at the pavement. I worried that she might be thinking of the very same stuff.

"Hey," I said, trying to make my voice sound jolly. "How about we go to the demo site on Ninety-third Street?"

"All right, I guess." She didn't sound enthusiastic, but once we arrived at the tall sheets of plywood that fenced off the demolition area, she started to perk up a little. The week before, Jeremy and I had found a loose board on one corner. Security around these places is shockingly slack. Every so often I consider writing the mayor of New York and letting him know what a shoddy job the demo crews are doing and that little kids could really get hurt, but that probably wouldn't be in our best interest.

We slipped inside. The site was a mess of rubble, of course. The tenement had a blazing fire a few weeks before and had burned down partway. The demolition crew knocked the rest of it down a little while after. There were some real gems scattered around. To date, we had scavenged the motors from a washing machine, a heap of bicycle chains, an old laptop that worked some of the time, half of a pair of handcuffs (no keys), and a really beautiful slab of marble.

One time, we ran into a young guy who was also hunting there. He looked totally normal. Nice button-down shirt and jeans. He said he liked to furnish his apartment with recycled items. I thought that was a very polite way of saying he was a garbage picker, just like us. He was a pretty friendly guy, and he did give us some advice about new demo sites and a warning about metal scavengers. He said that they we should watch out for them. They were really protective of their sites, because they made a living out of collecting stuff like copper pipes, brass valves, and aluminum heating coils and selling it to scrap metal dealers. He said that they weren't beyond using violence if they caught you on their sites. That scared the heck out of me, but it made Jeremy even more eager to go scavenging. She liked anything that might pose bodily danger.

Back home, we dumped our haul in my room. Mom wasn't home yet—she never gets home before six thirty—and Honey's back teeth were swimming she had to pee so badly, so first thing I did was take her for a walk. Honey is a pit bull that Mom found in front of our apartment building one evening. We named her Honey so that she wouldn't seem quite so scary to people, but it never really worked. In the elevator people press themselves up against the opposite wall and give her the evil eye. She doesn't seem to care. She wags her tail at them anyway. She's so easygoing that she never fusses when I put the Crap Catcher on her. It's one of my first inventions. Fairly primitive—a strap around the waist and a loop fitted under her butt, made of wire slipped into a sleeve of plastic. Attached to the loop is a tiny motor, scavenged from an electric shaver I found at a demo site on Seventy-seventh Street. What you do is you fasten a plastic bag around the loop with a rubber band and walk your dog. When she does her thing, you push one button on a handheld remote and the band cinches together quickly. The rubber band pings off the loop and the plastic bag falls to the ground, ready for you to pick up and put in the garbage can. It works beautifully. You wouldn't believe how many people stop me in the street and ask where they can buy one. The only weak spot is the rubber band pinging off somewhere.

After I walked Honey, I opened the fridge and found a plate on the bottom shelf with an apple, a slim slice of cheese, and a handful of zucchini sticks. My afternoon snack. I devoured it in two minutes flat. It made zero impact on the empty hole in my stomach where the three Oreos should have been.

I knew where the package of Oreos was kept. The cabinet above the refrigerator. My mom calls it the Stop-and-Think Cabinet. In order to reach it, you have to find the phone book and the dictionary, drag over a chair, put the phone book on the chair, the dictionary on top of the phone book, then balance yourself on top of the phone book and the dictionary in order to reach the shelf. All that dragging and balancing, and potentially falling, gives you time to stop and think if what's in that cabinet is really worth the trouble. It was. But here's the thing . . . let's say I did take a few unauthorized Oreo cookies. There was a chance that Mom wouldn't notice they were missing. But there was also a chance that she would. If she did, she wouldn't get mad. She wouldn't yell or anything like that. What she'd do was worse. She'd look me in the eye and tell me that I had broken my promise to her. *Pow*. That's like getting the worst sucker punch right in the gut. If you don't believe me, you don't know Mom.

Three more hours till dinner. I went to my room with a sickish rumbling in my stomach. In the center of the room was a tripod on which stood an eighteen-inch satellite dish. On the floor was a black receiver, an old television set, a mass of wire coils, connectors, and various hardware.

Her name is Nemesis.

I've been researching and building Nemesis for a year and a half. She's nearly finished.

I'm not going to tell you what she will do once she's complete. You don't know me well enough yet. You probably think you do. Everyone thinks they know the fat kid. We're so obvious. Our embarrassing secret is out there for everyone to see, spilling over our belts, flapping under our chins, stretching the seams of our jeans.

That doesn't mean we don't have other secrets that you can't see.

I pulled out the metal toolbox from under my bed and opened it. As always, I took a moment to admire the sight— neatly organized nuts, bolts, and screws in the top shelf, tiny to medium-sized wire clippers and an X-Acto knife in the middle shelf, and needle nose pliers, wire strippers, and screwdrivers in the bottom shelf, arranged according to size, along with bottles of oil and grease and an ancient soldering iron.

Thomas Edison once said, "To invent, you need a good imagination and a pile of junk."

I definitely had the junk. There was also a carton in my closet, full of old motors—motors from electric fans, automatic jewelry cleaners, and toy cars all the way up to a boat's outboard motor—tangles of wires, spare parts from the auto salvage, an elevator cable, and much more.

I sat down and started to work on Nemesis. When an hour flew I began to realize something alarming.

I could try her now.

After a year and half of researching and scavenging and tinkering, she was ready for a dry run. It made me feel squirrelly in my stomach. But maybe I was just hungry.

I switched her on, tuned the TV to Channel 37, a station which we don't get on our regular television. Then I waited. Nothing happened. I adjusted the angle of the Satellite dish a dozen times. Nothing.

Two more hours flew by. There was a quick knock at my door, and Mom popped her head in. I'll give you a description of Mom's head. She has heavy-lidded green eyes without many eyelashes, which is, unfortunately, very apparent due to her thick glasses. The glasses have pink frames. Her nose is . . . just a nose, nothing remarkable there. Her lips chap pretty easily. Her hair is blond and thin, and she often wears it in a short ponytail. You wouldn't notice her in a crowd. Or if you did, you might mistake her for the woman who makes appointments for you at the orthodontist's office.

It's her voice that is unusual. It's velvety. It brushes against your eardrum and slips down your ear canal and it makes you feel like everything will turn out okay, no matter how bad things look at the moment. Which is a good thing since Mom is a 911 dispatcher for the NYC Police Department.

Every year, she gets Christmas cards from people who have spoken to her on the 911 line, thanking her. They address the letters to The Woman with the Beautiful Voice or The Lady Who Sounds Like an Angel. The guy who distributes the mail always knows who they mean and he drops the cards on Mom's desk.

"What's cooking, good-lookin'?" she asked.

"Nothing much," I answered a little glumly.

"How's the radio thingy coming?"

She thinks Nemesis is a satellite radio. Well, she thinks that because I *told* her that. It was a lie. I also lied about where I got the parts. I told her I have a friend whose father owns a junk shop. She would be furious if she knew Jeremy and I were crashing demo sites.

"It needs work."

"It looks fine to me," she said. "Very . . . scientific."

"It doesn't matter how it looks. It has to work. And so far, it doesn't." I try to be patient with her.

"How was school?"

"Same old. How was work?"

"Same old."

We were both lying, of course. There was no way I was going to tell her how school was. It was too gruesome. And there was no way she was going to tell me how work was. Again, too gruesome. Although lately I think Jeremy gives her more anxiety than the stuff she hears at her job.

For instance, this was the conversation at dinner:

"How was the math test, Caitlin?" Mom asked Jeremy.

"It was fine, Zelda," Jeremy said.

They have this thing. Mom refuses to call her Jeremy. She thinks it's ridiculous. So Jeremy refuses to call her Mom and uses her real name instead.

It drives them both insane.

I try to stay out of it, though.

"You know, Owen," Mom said, "you look thinner."

I rolled my eyes.

"No, really," she said. "I see a difference. Around your face, I think."

"Watch, I'll probably only lose weight on my face," I said. "Then I'll have a tiny pinhead attached to a fat body."

"It doesn't work that way, Owen."

"He's being sarcastic, Zelda," Jeremy said.

"Besides," Mom said, attempting to ignore her, "you were thin once. I've seen the pictures. You were very well proportioned."

"Can we not talk about this?" I said.

Mom frowned and bit her lip. Then she said, "Oh, jeez. Sorry, honey. Of course."

She misunderstood. She thought it was the past I didn't want to talk about. Actually it was the fact that I had once been skinny. That embarrassed me. I felt like I had failed some tests along the way. Like I had started out with fine biological potential and through my own weakness had wrecked it. I still had a bag of my old clothes from two years ago sitting in the back of my closet. Normal-sized clothes. I should have dumped them, but I didn't want to. They reminded me of what I once was. The stupid thing was, though, I couldn't look at them either, because they reminded me of what I once was. Consequently, they just sat there, taking up too much space. Much like myself.

After dinner I flew through my homework, which was laughable, and took the elevator downstairs to apartment 5A. I pressed the buzzer, and in a minute the door was opened by a small, wiry man with skin the color of a Bit-O-Honey candy bar. This is Nima. He's Tibetan, but he grew up in India and only came to New York a few months ago.

"*Tashi-deley,*" he mouthed to me as he held a phone to his ear, and he nodded for me to come in. It was the dinkiest apartment you could imagine—one little room that served as a kitchen/dining room/living room/bedroom. You'd think that would be depressing, but it wasn't. In fact, it was a really cheerful place, with bright wall hangings, and colorful cloth draped over the couch and bed (which was just a thin mattress tucked into a corner of the room). On top of the television set were framed pictures of a very pretty woman. In one picture she wore a long blue dress with a striped apron hanging down from her waist, and in another she wore jeans and a white tank top. That was his new wife, Pema. I tried not to stare too much at her.

He had a little shrine on an end table in the corner, which was covered with a red, blue, and yellow cloth. On it was a statue of Buddha and a framed picture of the Dalai Lama, who is the leader of Tibet. Also, there were seven silver bowls filled with water, a bell, candles, and, depending on the day, a bunch of flowers or some pieces of fruit, which are offerings to the Buddha. Buddha doesn't eat them, of course. It's a Santa-and-the-milk-and-cookies kind of thing, without the presents or the ho, ho, ho. Although the Buddha definitely has that jolly fat man look about him.

I sat down on the couch and waited for Nima to finish his call. He was speaking in Tibetan, but I was pretty sure he was talking to Pema, who was still living in India, because he barely said anything, and when he did talk, he kept being cut off mid-sentence. He didn't get mad, though. It's really hard to ruffle Nima. When he hung up, he smiled at me.

"She have a hot temper," he said. He's secretly proud of that, I think, even though I'm under the impression that a hot temper is un-Buddhist.

"What's she mad about?"

"Oh, I went to party at her cousin's house in Brooklyn last week. Family party, such kind of thing. She heard I was flirting with her cousin."

"Were you?"

"Actually, it's possible." He smiled. His left front tooth is covered with gold, which makes him look like a very good-natured pirate. You could see how he might flirt with some girl without really trying. He's youngish, maybe twenty-one or twenty-two, something like that, and I bet girls would like him. He always looks like he's about to wink at you, though I've never seen him actually wink.

Nima made me some sweet tea and opened up a Tupperware container full of cold momos. Momos are Tibetan dumplings filled with meat and vegetables and garlic and other things. They are so good you could cry. Nima makes them by hand and sells them from a cart that he parks in front of the Museum of Natural History. We used to bump into each other in the elevator when I was walking Honey and he was coming back home from work. He was fascinated by the Crap Catcher and I was fascinated by the smell coming from his bag of leftover momos. It was a match made in heaven.

Today, as always, he asked me how Nemesis was coming along. Fine, fine, still needs some work, I said. He didn't know what Nemesis would do when it was finished. He once asked, back when I first met him.

"If I told you, you wouldn't believe me," I said.

"Perhaps not," he'd replied. That was that. He'd never asked again. But he liked hearing about it. He told me that when the Dalai Lama was a kid, he used to be able to fix movie projectors and clocks and cars and that if the Dalai Lama hadn't been the Dalai Lama, he would have been an engineer. I guess that puts me in pretty good company.

I didn't tell Nima about the thing with Mr. Wooly. It was just too humiliating. I did tell him about the missing Oreo cookies and Mason, though.

"You've got to see this kid. He's pure evil," I said.

"Hmm."

"Oh no. Are you going to tell me something Buddhist?" I said warily.

"You don't want to hear?" he asked, smiling.

"Not really. But go ahead."

"This boy, Mason, he is your enemy?"

"Well, he's stealing from me, so yeah, it's safe to say he's my enemy."

"Good," Nima said.

"How is that good?" I asked.

"Because enemies are very helpful. Better in some way than friends. If you stay calm when your enemy harms you, you become much stronger-type person."

I must have looked unimpressed because he added, "Also, it is good for your karma. You do good thing, good thing happen for you. You do bad thing—" He shook his head gravely. Then he smiled. It's hard for Nima to stay too serious.

"Fine," I said. "So I stay calm and think nice Buddhist thoughts about Mason. Then tomorrow he goes pawing through my lunch bag and takes my cookies again."

"Possibly you could leave a note," Nima said.

"A note?!" My voice grew shrill. "And what do you suggest I say?"

"You could say, 'Kindly not to take my cookies.'"

"Ha!" Sometimes Nima was very unrealistic. I think it came from him always assuming that people were sensible.

"Or maybe . . . actually . . ." He glanced at me as though he were about to suggest something he thought he shouldn't.

"What?" I asked.

"You could make a thing. Like your Crap Catcher. Only a Teef Catcher."

He had trouble with the *th* sound, so it took me a moment to realize that he meant "Thief Catcher."

I blinked.

"I could," I said.

"Just to prevent him from doing so again. Not harming him, of course."

"Of course not." I was liking the idea more and more with each passing minute.

Nima, on the other hand, looked more and more apprehensive. He was probably wondering if this suggestion was going to bring on some bad karma for me or something like that.

"But maybe you give this kid another chance. Maybe it was such kind of one-time mischief. Like flirting with your wife's cousin."

"Okay," I said. "I'll wait till tomorrow. I'll give him another chance. We'll see if it happens again."

4

It happened again. My three Oreos were gone. And the top of the eco-container was sealed tight. It felt like Mason Ragg was leaving me a message. Something like: *I can get in and out of your lunch so easily that I even have time to seal up your eco-container. And PS, an eco-container is very hard to seal. You are powerless against me.*

Maybe that sounds paranoid to you. You'll see, though, that it wasn't.

When I got home that afternoon, I put aside my work on Nemesis and started working on my new idea right away. It had to be small and inconspicuous. And lethal.

Just kidding.

I only wanted it to inflict a moderate amount of pain.

I rummaged through my cardboard box and pulled out the half a handcuff that Jeremy and I had found. It looked like someone had managed to smash the chain link between the two manacles. Why they did that, I have no idea. Jeremy suggested that the person may have been handcuffed to a top secret briefcase, like you see on old movies, and a thief had smashed the chain to get it away from him. Seemed far-fetched, but who knows. Anyway, I always wanted to use it for something, but I'd never had an opportunity before now. I pulled out my yellow graph paper notebook and my mechanical pencil and began to draw my plans. When I was satisfied, I dug around through my box and found a spring from the hood latch of an old Buick, a Swiss Army knife, and a dog collar with some very nasty spikes on it. I opened my toolbox and pulled out my trusty soldering iron, and I borrowed a tiny sewing kit from Mom's desk.

By the time I was finished, I had lined my lunch sack with a mechanism that looked like it had come straight out of the Spanish Inquisition. Spiked handcuffs, high-tensile springs. I dubbed it the Jaws of Anguish. It was genius. I actually felt sorry for Mason. I imagined him shrieking in pain as the Jaws of Anguish snapped tight around his wrist, my sack of lunch attached to his hand. Teachers would poke their heads out in the hallway. Busted. Immediate suspension. If there was such a thing at our school.

I called up Izzy and told him my plan, fully expecting him to be as excited as I was.

"I don't know, Owen," he said guardedly.

"What? Come on, it's perfect!" I said.

"Yeah, but you're dealing with Mason Ragg, dude. The guy is capable of anything. Do you really want to be pulling that particular tiger's tail?"

"Well, I have to do something," I said.

But once I was lying there in bed, in the dark, I kept imagining Mason's face . . . scarred, evil, and really, *really* angry.

I almost lost my nerve. By morning, though, the prospect of being carved up by Mason's switchblade seemed less likely. Slightly.

I checked the Jaws of Anguish several times that morning using a section of old pipe as a "wrist." It worked like a dream.

That morning I sat at the math station with Rachel Lowry, the girl who looked like she might be in GWAB but wasn't, and Aidan Overbeck, who is as hyper as a gerbil and about as intelligent. His leg never stopped jiggling as he tried to work out an equation. He was making the entire math workstation jiggle too until Rachel finally clamped her hand on his knee and squeezed hard. Aidan squealed (much like a gerbil) and said, "What was that for?" And Rachel said, "You are a one-man earthquake." And he said something idiotic like, "It's better than being a one-woman ugly." It was so stupid that Rachel didn't even bother to roll her eyes. I sort of like her.

While I was working on a math problem, I kept glancing over at Mason. He caught me once and his twisted mouth stretched into an expression that was hard to define. When half a person's face is all messed up like that, it's really had to tell if that person is smiling at you or scowling. I was thinking it probably wasn't a smile. I attempted to shoot back a cool, stony stare, but I couldn't quite manage it and wound up shrugging at him and going, "Heesh." I have no idea why. He looked away with what I assume was disgust. Again, hard to tell.

At 11:07, Mason got up from the global studies station, quickly walked to the front of the room, and got the bathroom pass from Ms. Bussle. My heart started thumping. My veins were crawling with adrenaline. This is what it feels like to be powerful, I thought. This is the revenge feeling. It was so different from the squashed feeling I usually felt at school. The victim feeling. Why hadn't I thought to use my brains for combat before this? All those times when I'd been humiliated . . . when my hair had been set on fire during assembly and when a girl had stuck pins in me to see if I bled brown because of all the chocolate I ate. I might have had revenge back then.

"Nima won't like this."

That was the little voice in my head speaking.

Sometimes little voices in your head should be ignored.

I waited and listened. There might be a yelp of surprise or a howl of anger. I looked around for a weapon, just in case I had to defend myself. It was slim pickings, but I spotted a protractor compass in a tray in front of Rachel and casually picked it up. One side was a pointy metal stick. That would do. I pretended to measure some arcs, my eyes flitting to the door every other second. He was taking forever. Finally the door opened. Mason walked in. There was no lunch sack attached to his hand. He didn't look angry. In fact, he looked sort of calm.

Again, hard to tell with his face being what it was.

I put down the protractor compass and rushed up to Ms. Bussle.

"Bathroom pass," I said breathlessly.

"A please would be nice."

"Please."

I hurried out the door to the sounds of snide giggles from my classmates, who must have thought I was having a urinary emergency. I didn't care. I ran to the wide, door-less closet that was recessed in the wall a few yards from my classroom. There were rows of hooks where we kept our coats and backpacks, and above that was the shelf on which our lunches sat. My lunch sack was where I left it. It looked untouched. Very carefully, with my right hand supporting the bottom, I took it off the shelf. Putting it on the floor, I peered inside. The spiked handcuff was in place, open and poised against the side of the sack. Directly below it was the eco-container.

The cookies were gone.

I took the thick wooden-dowel bathroom pass and inserted it in the sack, then pried the edge of the eco-container with it. *Snick!* The cuff snapped closed on the imaginary wrist, just as it was supposed to, and I slipped the dowel out. There was no way Mason could have by-passed the mechanism . . . yet he had!

I heard footsteps down the hallway, so I replaced my lunch sack on the shelf and made a quick stop at the bathroom, just to complete my alibi. I actually had to go anyway.

When I got back to the classroom, I automatically searched out Mason. He had planted himself in the global studies workstation and was tattooing his forearm with a green felt-tip marker.

I usually just suck things up. I don't complain, I don't start trouble. I'm good at that. Lots of practice.

But when people steal things from me, I have to do something about it. Two years ago something was stolen from me—the biggest thing you could possibly steal from a person, really, apart from their life—and Nemesis was hopefully going to help me make things right on that account.

Now Mason Ragg had stolen from me too. Three times. I couldn't suck it up. I walked right up to Mason and stood over him with my hands on my hips.

"Give them back," I hissed.

He looked up from his tattooing. Unfortunately, I was standing by the messed-up side of his face, so that when he looked up I was staring full on at the misshapen sneer and the milky blue eye. It actually made me gulp, which is one of those things that characters do in books but that never happen in real life. Except when Mason Ragg looks at you with the messed-up side of his face. Then all those things that you read about in books but never happen in real life—

like hair standing up on the back of your neck or shaking in your boots or gulping—are suddenly entirely possible.

"Give what back?" he snarled.

"You know what." I was trying to avoid saying it because it sounded sort of ridiculous, but Mason just kept staring me down with that lunar blue eyeball, so I was forced to say, "Give me back my cookies."

"Your *cookies*?" he snorted. "What would I want with your *cookies*?"

If you say the word *cookie* in a sneering way, it can sound an awful lot like a preschool term—like *binky* or *blankey*.

"Look," I said, "I know it was you. You took them yesterday and the day before and, though I don't know how you managed it, you took them again today. Just give them back, all right . . . just . . ."—I thrust my open palm out toward him—"give them back and I won't tell on you."

Then Mason said something that I can't repeat.

I stood there for a minute feeling especially fat. I mean, I always feel fat, but sometimes I feel like a boulder. A huge fat boulder that people write curse words on or pee on. And I just stand there, letting it happen, because I'm a boulder and that's what boulders do.

Boulders also turn around and walk away from people who terrify them, which is also exactly what I did.

Jeremy would have stood her ground even if it meant getting thrashed. Even if it meant a switchblade in the gut. I winced at the thought.

Behind my back, I heard Mason hiss at me, "You're not as smart as you think you are."

That stopped me cold. I felt a sickening, swirling feeling in my stomach. Remember when you were a little kid and you wouldn't let your feet dangle from the bed because you were afraid a monster might grab your ankle, pull you under the bed, and eat your intestines? Logically, you knew it probably would never happen, but still, there was that little speck of doubt.

Hearing Mason Ragg say, "You're not as smart as you think you are," was like being pulled under the bed by the monster. And having my intestines eaten. "Not being as smart as I think I am" was something that I often worried about as I worked on Nemesis. It nagged at me when I measured trajectories, when I was splicing wires or soldering parts. Could I really do this? Was I *really* as smart as I thought I was? Then I'd think logically. My IQ is . . . well, I'm not allowed to tell you what it is, but believe me, it's impressive. I could do it. I had to do it.

Then along comes Mason Ragg, evil comic-book character/bogyman who figures out a way to bypass the Jaws of Anguish and then tells me that I'm not as smart as I think I am.

"I don't feel well."

Ms. Bussle looked at me from her desk in that squinty, nearsighted way she has.

"What's wrong, Owen?"

"Nauseous," I mumbled.

"Did you eat something you shouldn't have?" she asked. By the way, she has a loud voice.

"Like the state of Texas?" one kid said.

"Like a mastodon?" another kid called out.

"Here. Go to the nurse," Ms. Bussle said, quickly giving me the hall pass. She'd started something that she knew she wouldn't be able to stop.

"Like a Twinkie factory?"

5

The nurse, a pear-shaped woman with a pointy nose, took my temperature but barely glanced at the thermometer. She seemed to know it would read normal.

"Bad day?" she asked.

"I'm feeling nauseous," I told her.

I needed to leave the school. Now. I had things to do.

She did a little sniffing thing where her lips pushed out and her nose wrinkled. She was considering. Or else she had highly developed olfactory senses that could sniff out when kids were lying to her. Either way, she decided in my favor.

"All right, let's give Mom a call." She pulled up the information from her computer and dialed. Mom couldn't leave work—she's usually in the middle of dealing with some hairy situation—but she sent over Mrs. Leaper, an elderly neighbor, to come fetch me from school then leave me alone in our apartment.

In my room, I carefully removed the Jaws of Anguish

from my lunch sack and ate the sandwich. After that I ate my snack in the fridge.

The phone rang. It was Mom.

"How's the belly?"

"Not so good." I tried to make my voice sound weak and shaky, which wasn't hard.

"Have you vomited?" she asked. Her voice was professionally level, but I could hear the anxiety seeping through.

"Not yet," I answered as I stood by the kitchen window and stared at Andre's apartment building, the Fuji Towers. It was directly across the street, a slick steel-and-glass apartment building with a steeply angled scooped-out steel roof on one side, like a giant snowplow had been nailed onto the side of the building. It was insanely ugly, but it probably was supposed to be very chic or something.

"Peppermint tea," she said.

"Okay."

"In little sips."

"Yeah."

"You'll be fine."

"I know."

She might have been talking to one of her callers. "Stay calm. Deep breaths. Help is on the way."

I ate another PB&J, a bowl of cereal, and a hunk of cheddar cheese. I scaled the chair and phone book and the dictionary to the Stop-and-Think Cabinet without stopping to think, and I grabbed five Oreos out of the package and devoured them in less time than it took me to get them. I'd be sorry later, I knew, when Mom discovered it, but it seemed totally worth it. After the cookies were finished, I had second thoughts, but of course it was too late to do anything about it.

That was why I climbed back up and ate seven more.

After that, I turned on Nemesis and got down to work—adjusting the dish, trying different channels. Nothing happened. Mason's words started replaying in my brain. I tried to beat them back. I told myself that I was attempting to do something extraordinary, something that a thug like Mason would never be able to do. But staring at a blank TV screen for an hour was beginning to wear away at my confidence.

Then I heard a voice.

It was coming from my TV set.

There was a picture too, but it was so fuzzy I couldn't make out anything. Still, I could hear someone talking about a tractor.

I must be picking up some farming channel.

I yelled and punched the air and did this little dance, but that part was embarrassing so I stopped doing it pretty fast.

My equipment worked!

But not well.

And it was going to have to work very, *very* well in order for Nemesis to do what I needed it to do.

I was going to have to boost the signal, which meant I needed an amplifier. Forty decibel or better.

I emptied out my backpack, slung it over my shoulder, and headed for the demolition site on West Eighty-second Street, between Broadway and Amsterdam Avenue. Jeremy had told me about it. She had spotted it when she was on her way to a GWAB member's house. She said that it was impressive: three old tenements that had been knocked down to make way for a high-rise condominium. Ripe hunting grounds for an amplifier.

I walked down Broadway, on the west side of the street. Broadway was livelier than Amsterdam Avenue. In fact, it reminded me of a kid with ADD, all hopped up and in constant motion. Even the stores couldn't stay focused for very long. A new restaurant would open, then close a few months later, reopen again as a clothing store, then close again and reopen, close and reopen. I peered into a new stereo and electronics shop, its shelves full of slippery black equipment. It was almost as alluring to me as the Italian bakery on the block before. For now, though, I'd have to be satisfied with what I scavenged.

When I reached Eighty-fifth Street, I almost crossed over to the east side of Broadway. It was an involuntary reflex. I hadn't been by the store in months, and I didn't know if I wanted to see it today when I wasn't feeling too terrific about myself.

I made myself do it, though. I kept walking on the west

side of the street. My heart began to race, stomping crazily like the feet of a rabbit that's been picked up by the scruff of its neck and is struggling to get away.

"Breathe," I said, just like Mom to one of her callers. "You'll be fine."

A stationary store. A hair salon. *Breathe.* A magazine and smoke shop, the same one that had been there for as long as I could remember. The owner, he—shhh. *Breathe.*

I made myself stop when I reached the shoe store. I must have looked funny—standing still in the middle of the street like that, not looking at the store I was stopped in front of but straight ahead—because a few people glanced at me. Okay, I said to them in my head. Fine. I'll look. You're making me look.

The store was completely different than it once had been, of course. There were the shoes, for one thing. Sleek, expensive-looking shoes for men. Dark and polished. On one wall were sandals and some colorful sneakers, but the colors were odd, like acid green and orange. I didn't know any men who wore shoes like this. My father had always worn battered canvas loafers.

As always, it wasn't the differences that struck me so much as what had remained the same. There was the same ancient, white-painted tin ceiling, made up of dozens of embossed squares. There was the narrow door in the back wall, behind the cash register; that was the door that led to a short hallway. On one side of the hallway was a dinky little office. On the other side was the door to the basement.

The walls had been repainted. Of course.

The store was empty except for a balding blond man, very spiffily dressed in a gray suit. He looked a little bored. His hands were in his pockets, and he was staring at a row of shoes with strange, squared-off toes, as though he was trying to decide if he liked them or not, without really seeming to care much either way. He turned away from the square-toed shoes and scratched the back of his neck. The scratching turned into picking at something, maybe a pimple or a scab.

Out of the corner of my eye, I caught sight of someone staring at me through the window of the magazine and smoke shop next door. The graying hair was slicked back and oiled with pomade, and I could see the flash of gold around his neck. Mr. Boscana. I shouldn't have been surprised to see him. He'd been sitting at that same stool behind the counter for as long as I could remember. Still, the sight of that familiar face jolted me. I could read a quick series of emotions playing with his features—shock, pity. He collected himself and rearranged his mouth into a wide, warm smile, his white teeth flashing even behind the smudged window. He rose from his stool by the cash register.

In a minute he was standing outside his store, his necklace and teeth flashing in the sun. "Owen! Owen, *mi hombrecito!*"

I'm a coward. You know that about me already. For the second time in a single day, I chickened out. This time was worse than the time with Mason. This time I heard the hurt in Mr. Boscana's voice, calling after me as I rushed away down the street: "Owen!! Hang on a minute!"

The liveliness of Broadway now felt like some menacing barricade. I couldn't maneuver through the crowds. People seemed to be deliberately squeezing together too tightly, just to keep a fat kid from passing them. Finally I shoved my way between a couple. My body touched theirs. People don't often make physical contact in New York City, even though we are all pressed together so tightly. It almost always produces a strong reaction.

"Watch where you're going!" the man said.

"Big oaf!" the woman muttered.

Big oaf. Big oaf. The sound of that played back in my head as I ran across the wide street and east, away from Broadway and the crowds. Big oafs were frightening. Big oafs were the mean, sweating guys dressed in Speedos tossing other big oafs into the air inside pro-wrestling cages. Why wasn't I that sort of oaf? Why wasn't I that sort of fat?

Because you are the boulder. Boulders just sit there and let people do what they want.

All of a sudden I didn't care about the demolition site anymore. I didn't care about the forty-decibel amplifier.

I didn't even care about Nemesis anymore.

The only thing I cared about at that moment was that I was starving. It was a sudden burning, aching hunger that left me dizzy. The empty space in my gut where the three

Oreo cookies should have been had doubled, tripled, despite everything that I had eaten back home. I dug through my pockets, but all I found were two dimes. Not enough for anything. I counted the blocks that I'd have to walk to get back home: eleven. Too far.

But Nima's momo cart was only three and a half blocks away.

6

I crossed over to Columbus Avenue and then walked a few blocks downtown to the Museum of Natural History. There were three or four people in line at Nima's cart, which stood to the left of the wide steps that led up to the museum entrance. Hanging by a cord around the front of the cart were brightly colored flags, and printed on the red awning were the words NIMA'S AUTHENTIC HANDMADE MOMOS. Nima was behind his cart, as small as a kid and so skinny. I could see his hands furiously working away at forming his dumplings and dropping them in the huge steamer pot. My stomach responded to the sight by cramping with hunger. I walked faster.

"Owen!" Nima spotted me even as he toiled away. He smiled, then looked confused, although his hands never stopped working. "Why you not in school?"

The other people in line looked at me too.

"I got out early," I told him. Not a lie really. My eyes

anxiously flitted to the dumplings that he had just pulled out of the steamer with a spider spatula. Nima noticed—he noticed everything—and he plunked a half dozen of the dumplings on a paper plate, squeezed out some dipping sauce from a squeeze bottle into a little paper cup and handed them to me. This produced some grumbling from the line of people, and one of them actually walked away.

"No worry, no worry," Nima assured the rest of the people in line, smiling in his good-natured way. "I work fast. Not wait long time." His small hands worked even faster. At any other time I would have felt very guilty. But today I didn't care. I sat on the steps of the museum and devoured the dumplings in minutes. I was still hungry afterward, but I felt better.

Gradually, the lunch rush dwindled and then stopped altogether. Nima came over and sat beside me on the steps. He pulled a pack of cigarettes out of his pocket, shook one out, and lit it. I probably shouldn't mention that he smokes because it gives a bad impression of him, but he's trying to quit and anyway, it's his business.

"So crazy at lunchtime!" he said after blowing out some smoke and glancing at me with his bright, dark eyes. "I need two more hands, I'm thinking. But I can't afford to pay two more hands. So here's my plan: I make momos with my feet. I have nice, long toes. Wiggly nice. I keep them clean. Not even hairy. Smooth as Pema's cheek. The cheek up top, I mean. What do you think?" He kept a perfectly serious face. It took me months before I could tell when he was joking. When I first met him, I just thought he was a little insane.

"I think the Board of Health would take away your cart," I said dryly.

I was in no mood for jokes.

Nima took another drag from his cigarette and shook his head solemnly.

"Probably right, probably right."

We were quiet for a while, but he kept stealing glances over at me. It made me feel a little squirmy. There's a lot Nima doesn't know about me, and in quiet moments I feel like he's trying to figure me out.

"I was heading down to a demolition site," I told him, just to end the quiet moment. "A big one. Lots of great junk there. I'm looking for one more thing in order to get Nemesis working the way I need her to."

"Jeremy is going to help you?" he asked.

"She's in school," I said, then remembered I had said that school got out early, sort of. He didn't let on that he'd caught me at my lie. He just nodded thoughtfully and took another drag from his cigarette. By the way, I have never seen Nima eat. I know he must, but I've never seen it. The only thing I know for sure about his eating habits is that he doesn't eat shrimp. He told me that once. "Too many shrimp have to die in order to fill just one belly." That's true, of course. But he doesn't know what he's missing.

A customer came up to his cart, so he darted away for a

few moments. While he was gone, I watched a woman place a rubber mat down on the sidewalk in front of the museum. On the mat she placed a portable CD player. She was wearing a long dress with every conceivable color swirling though it. Looped around her neck was a long yellow scarf. She pressed a button on the CD player and some fast, whiny music started to blare. Spreading her arms wide, she began to spin in a circle, the way little kids do sometimes. It looked totally ridiculous. She was clearly a nut job. Still, I couldn't take my eyes off her. The colors on her dress melted together as she spun, faster and faster. The air around her seemed to change, as though her edges were bleeding into their molecules. If she spins much faster, I thought, she'll break apart and disappear.

"She come here every day and dance like that," Nima said as he sat back down beside me.

"I thought she was just a crazy person," I said.

"Oh, yes, she very crazy person." He smiled as though he approved. "But she always look happy. So . . . what more she need?"

I shrugged. "I guess nothing, if she's happy."

"Oh no, no." Nima laughed. "Not *she*." He nodded toward the woman, who was now beginning to slow down. "I mean Nemesis. What more she need in order to work better?"

"A certain kind of amplifier. I have a receiver, but I have to boost the signal to make sure it comes in strong enough. What I'm trying to do is very complicated. No one has ever done it before. At least, they didn't *know* they were doing it, so it amounts to the same thing." I felt a rush of excitement as I spoke about Nemesis. I had only ever spoken about her like this to Jeremy.

"I don't understand," Nima said, tapping out another cigarette from his pack. "How the other people not know what they do when they build something like a Nemesis?"

"Because they *didn't* build it. It was something that happened accidentally."

Nima took a drag on his cigarette and nodded. Most people would have pried at that point, but not Nima. He understood about people's secrets.

But today, for some reason, I wanted to tell him. Not everything. Not yet. Just a little bit.

"That's how I first got the idea for Nemesis, actually. There's this show on TV called *Skeptical Minds,* where scientists investigate supernatural stuff, like ghost sightings and UFOs. Nine times out of ten they prove that the story was all nonsense. Well, I had the show on, but I wasn't paying that much attention when all of a sudden something caught my eye. One of the places where ghosts had been spotted was The Black Baron Pub."

"This the same pub right next to our apartment building?"

"The very same. It turns out the guy who owns the pub had a wireless surveillance camera in there that kept capturing these weird, fuzzy images of people milling around while the place was closed on Sunday. But there was no sign of break-ins, and nothing was ever missing. He said that when he bought the place three years ago, he had heard some stories about the building being haunted, but he thought it was a lot of nonsense. Now he was beginning to think it was true. So these scientists tested his story right on TV. They checked his surveillance camera and receiver to make sure it wasn't rigged, and they hid in a backroom on a Sunday night, watching. They didn't see a thing. But when they checked the surveillance camera recording in the morning, there were those fuzzy-looking people, milling around. You couldn't make out faces or clothes or anything, but they were definitely people. You could only see them for a few minutes, and when they were gone, the place looked completely empty again. It totally stumped the scientists. It almost stumped me too. I mean, it really seemed like this guy had ghosts in his pub."

"Ah." Nima nodded. I waited for him to scoff at the notion. Or at least make a joke. He didn't. He just listened, looking down at the spot between his black sneakers, frowning in concentration.

"You don't really believe in ghosts, do you?" I asked him.

"Oh, sure, sure. Unhappy spirit. Tibetans call such kind of thing Hungry Ghost. It is very unfortunate to be a Hungry Ghost."

Once in a while it was disappointing to hear Nima's beliefs.

"Of course the guy didn't *actually* have ghosts in his pub," I said. "There are no such things as ghosts. When people die, they are just gone."

Nima looked at me but said nothing. No, not looked at me. He watched me. His cigarette drooped between his narrow, brown fingers, forgotten for a few moments. He was thinking, not about the TV show, I was pretty sure, but about me. It made me uncomfortable, and he seemed to realize it suddenly. He took a puff on his cigarette and nodded, his eyes averted. I went on.

"Like I said, I was stumped at first. But they replayed those surveillance recordings several times as they were interviewing the pub owner, and that was when I noticed something strange. In the recordings, you could see out one of the windows to the opposite side of the street, where Fuji Towers is. You know how there is that twenty-four-hour supermarket on the ground floor of Fuji Towers? The one with the giant tomato sign?"

"Sure, sure."

"Well, when you saw the ghost figures in the surveillance recording, the supermarket wasn't there. All you could see was scaffolding and the outline of the giant tomato-shaped sign. The supermarket was being built. But when the ghost figures went away and it was just a dark, empty pub again, you could see the supermarket in the background, totally built and lit up, with people coming in and out."

Nima shook his head. "Something wrong with the videotapes?"

"There were no tapes. They were digital recordings. The scientists checked out all the equipment, and there were no problems."

"So, how can be?" Nima asked.

"That's what I wondered. I asked Mom about when the supermarket was built, and she said it had been built two years ago. So, here's where things get real interesting. Have you ever taken a really good look at Fuji Towers? Have you ever looked at its roof?"

"It a funny shape," Nima said, making a scooping motion with his hand.

"Exactly. It's shaped like a giant parabolic dish, like a satellite dish. And it's steel, which makes it a perfect reflector of radio waves. It's like an accidental radio telescope. And it's facing The Black Baron Pub. What if, I wondered, the radio waves from The Black Baron Pub's surveillance camera hit the Fuji Tower's roof, were reflected off into space, where a star reflected them right back, and the camera's receiver captured them again? Since those images might have originally been caught on the surveillance camera when the pub was open, you *would* see people walking around. That made perfect sense. And because the reflected signal is weak, the people would look all fuzzy and you'd only be able to see them for a few minutes at a time. That also made perfect sense. What didn't make perfect sense was this: in order for a radio wave to come back to earth two years after it's been sent off into space, it has to bounce off a star that's only one light-year away. But the closest known star system, Alpha Centauri, is about four light years away. So I started doing research, and I found something interesting. Some astronomers believe that there is this red dwarf star which rotates around our sun. They call it Nemesis, and they believe it's only about one light-year away from earth. That's incredibly close. No one knows where this star is located exactly, but I have a hunch that the roof of Fuji Towers is pointed directly at it, and The Black Baron Pub directly faces the roof of Fuji Towers. That's why those images from the past came through on the surveillance camera." I paused. Here was the beauty part.

"Our apartment building faces the roof of the Fuji Towers too."

Nima nodded. He was trying not to look confused.

"The thing is, I want . . . I *need* to see a particular thing that happened in the past," I explained to him. "Something that happened almost two years ago."

"At Black Baron Pub?" he asked, still confused.

"No, no. Somewhere else."

"So your machine Nemesis," Nima said slowly, "she will show a moment that have already passed?"

"With the help of the Fuji Towers roof, yes."

There was a pause during which I waited, not breathing, for him to ask the question that I desperately didn't want him to ask:

What was that moment?

A slow smile twisted up one side of his mouth.

"What?" I asked nervously.

"Maybe Nemesis can show me at Pema's cousin's house last week, looking most depressed. Looking like so." He cupped his chin in his hand and looked most depressed.

I smiled. "And we'll show it to Pema."

"And she will weep with happiness."

7

After I left Nima, I was in a much better mood. My stomach had lost that empty feeling, and the sound of Mr. Boscana's voice was no longer ringing in my ears. I decided to go to visit the demolition site after all. It was a big one. You could tell it was a brand new site because the plywood fence around it was still a pale yellowish color and there were no posters taped to it or things scrawled on it. I walked around it once, scoping it out casually. Then I walked to the end of the block, turned around, and walked by it again slowly, this time letting my hand drag along the wooden fence. I put pressure on the boards at every seam to see if there was any give. There wasn't. In a way I was relieved. I'd never scavenged without Jeremy before. I wasn't entirely sure I had the guts to do it alone.

Just as I had satisfied myself that that there was no way in and had passed by the final board, I noticed something off to my right. Next to the demolition site was a community garden with a six-foot chain-link fence around it. The high wooden slabs of the demolition fence butted up against the chain-link fence, all except for one spot toward the back. The wooden fence hadn't quite been long enough to reach the length of the site, and since there was already a chain-link fence right there, they hadn't bothered to close off the foot-wide section.

I hesitated. It would mean scaling the chain-link fence, then trying to squeeze through the opening. I had images of myself being wedged between the wooden board and the adjacent building and of firefighters arriving to pry me free. Or worse, if someone called 911 and Mom found out about it. I started to walk past, then stopped again, stared at the opening. I could fit. I'd have to suck in my stomach and do some wiggling, but I was fairly sure I could get in there. What if there was an amplifier just sitting there? I had to try. I would be ashamed of myself if I didn't.

I opened the gate to the community garden and walked in. There wasn't much of anything growing at this time of year, just some odds-and-ends flowers and weeds. There was garbage too, probably tossed into it from the tenement building next door. People can be such pigs when they think no one's looking.

I walked to the back of the garden, and I took one quick look around. No one. Then I glanced up at the tenement building, but the way the sun was hitting its side, I couldn't make out much inside the windows. I took a deep breath and started to climb. As you might have guessed, I'm not much of a climber. I made a huge racket what with the fence jangling against the post and my foot slipping once so that I yelped like a dog whose paw had been stepped on. Swinging myself over the fence was a fumbling "oof—oh, crap—ouch" production. It's amazing that I didn't have the entire 20th police precinct circling me by the end of it.

On the other side of the fence, I squeezed between the wooden board and the building, and let me tell you, it took some major breath-holding. There was one point where the edges of the board held me in a vise, pinching my belly and my butt so hard I thought for sure I'd have to start screaming for help. But then I had visions of Winnie the Pooh stuck in Rabbit's hole and all his woodland friends pulling his paws to uncork him. I have no woodland friends. The best I could hope for was a couple of snickering pedestrians poking at me with Zabar's baguettes. I sucked in my breath harder, wiggled, and, finally, I was through.

The place was amazing! A field of rubble, studded with treasure: microwaves, sink tops, an exercise bike, several floor lamps, a shower stall, a bunch of computers, five dining room chairs, a dog kennel, three air conditioners, four vacuum cleaners, a mountain bike in mint condition except for a flat front tire, a beautiful spill of wires and cables, and so much more. It took my breath away. Fully half of one of the tenements still stood. It looked like it had been chopped in two by a giant's ax, and the giant had smashed the front half to bits but left the back half alone. You could see right into the ruined rooms, with curtains still hanging, televisions still sitting on their stands, but everything dark and gloomy. All that talk of ghosts with Nima now gave me the heebie-jeebies. I could imagine one of those fuzzy figures in The Black Baron Pub recording walking through those rooms, pausing to pull aside the filthy, tattered curtains, then settling on a broken chair. It made me goose pimply, so I told myself I was an idiot, opened my backpack, pulled out my tools, and got down to work.

Before a half hour was up, I had managed to fill my backpack. I even found a silver ice-skate charm for Jeremy, who happened to be a stellar ice skater, and a set of brand-new ratchets for myself. Still, nowhere in that mess of rubble was an amplifier. I left my heavy backpack on the ground and moved closer to the half-standing tenement. That was where there were some thicker piles of brick and mortar chunks. Crouching low, I pushed away rubble to inspect what was underneath.

That was when I heard the loud plink-plinking noise. It sounded like it was coming from an enormous wind chime. I froze where I was, kneeling on a knoll of bricks, listening. The sound came again, and this time I was fairly certain it was from inside the still-standing, sliced-in-half tenement.

My instinct was to make a run for it, but I had left my backpack several yards away, in the opposite direction of the hole in the fence. It would take me too long to scramble over the wreckage, retrieve my backpack, then squeeze myself out through the fence again. I estimated that it was better to hunker down and wait to see what was coming. Hopefully, the person wouldn't notice me amidst the piles of debris. Then my mind began to stray back to the image of the ghost passing through the rooms.

The plink-plinking came again, louder this time, and I tell you, I nearly fainted from fear. The fact that I didn't makes me think that it must be amazingly difficult to faint from fear.

I saw no figure of ghostly light. Instead, a figure of darkness appeared within the depths of the ruined tenement's third floor. It was black and bent, a giant bug with massive feelers stretched out in all directions. Mom had once been to Puerto Rico and she told me that she had seen cockroaches the size of kittens. They had nothing on this thing. It shuffled along, disappearing behind the exposed beams, keeping in the shadows, plinking as it moved.

I couldn't run now even if I wanted to. I was paralyzed with terror.

Then I saw the others.

There were two more of these bug things, creeping along in the shadows, their feelers extended. It was too much for me. I couldn't hunker any more. I bolted back to my knapsack, snatched it up, and ran, not caring that my backpack was plinking like mad.

Oh. My knapsack was plinking.

Much like the giant cockroaches. Which meant they were probably hauling scavenged items, same as I was.

I was at the fence when I realized this. I stopped and turned around, looking up at the tenement's third floor.

From my present angle, I couldn't see very well into the interior, but it didn't matter. One of the giant cockroaches was standing a few yards away from me, having just emerged from the bottom floor of the tenement. He was staring at me with an alarmed look on his face. He did have a face. It was filthy and bearded. He shifted his weight, and his feelers plink-plinked. They were made of old metal pipes that were sticking out of a sack strapped to his back. Most were lead, but some were copper, which fetched a tidy sum at the scrap-metal dealers.

Just as I remembered the words of that young, nicely dressed guy at the Ninety-third Street demo site— how the metal scavengers weren't beyond using violence to protect their territory—the figure held something up for me to see. He had been holding it in his hands the whole time, but I had been so focused on his face and feelers that I hadn't noticed it. It was a large bronze-colored sheet of metal with tiny white rectangles all over it. I stared at the thing. It was so oddly familiar. Then I realized what it was. The cover of the building's mailboxes. The metal scavenger had ripped it off the wall. I could see the names on those little rectangular pieces of paper: Tess Bailhouse, J. Rodriguez, R. S. Anderson, Robert/Shelly Weinstein . . . I might have some of their stuff in my backpack. Bits and scraps of their lives. It made me feel ooky. It made me feel like one of those grave robbers who dig up caskets and slip the wedding rings off dead people's fingers.

The scrap metal scavenger glanced at my backpack, sagging and lumpy with my loot. He smiled at me with brown teeth, and he raised his eyebrows.

"We done all right," he said, giving the mailbox cover a proud shake. He wasn't alarmed anymore. He had taken my measure and had decided I was on his team.

That made me feel even ookier.

I squeezed through the opening in the fence and climbed the garden fence in about two minutes, no wiggling, no stumbling. I don't know how I did it.

By the time I got home, Jeremy was already there with her friend Arthur.

"Hey, where were you?" Jeremy said. "We waited outside the school for, like, twenty minutes."

They were sitting at the kitchen table with an open notebook in front of Arthur, who was scribbling something in it.

"I didn't feel well," I said. "I left school early." I didn't want to talk about my day. It had been too strange.

Jeremy scrutinized me. "You don't look sick," she said.

"I feel better now."

"Good. We're furious," Jeremy said. "Aren't we furious, Arthur?"

"We are totally . . ." Arthur stopped writing for a moment and searched for the right word. "Furious."

Arthur is the president of GWAB. She actually does look like a boy, and it's not just because she has her hair cut short with tiny sideburns showing or because of the red polo shirt and chinos she always wears. She has a sort of heavy, bully-boy jaw. I think that makes the difference. Jeremy could cut her hair as short as Arthur's, but she would just look like a girl with short hair.

"What happened?" I asked. "Oh, was it Shackly? I told you he wouldn't go for the name thing."

"He says we have to retake the test tomorrow, and if we don't write our girl names on our tests, he's going to mark them with Fs! And that test is 50 percent of our entire grade!" Jeremy said. She was all bright-eyed. It was partly from anger, I'm sure, but I think it was partly from pure joy. She loved stuff like this. Fighting for hopeless causes.

"He *will* fail you guys, you know," I warned them.

"Let him." Jeremy smiled. "Mr. Shackly is going to be in for a little surprise tomorrow."

I looked at the two of them. Arthur was writing away in the notebook.

"What are you two doing?" I asked suspiciously.

"Oh, we're just drafting an e-mail, that's all," Jeremy said. She jabbed Arthur in the ribs and Arthur snorted and nodded. "Yes, just a simple e-mail," Jeremy continued. "Which Arthur is going to send to all the major television networks tonight. We think the news shows will be very interested to know about this situation."

I sincerely doubted that, but I didn't want to be the one to burst their bubble.

"Arthur will be our television spokesperson, of course,"

Jeremy went on to explain. That was even more dubious, since Arthur generally never said more than a few words at a time. "We're actually hoping that she gets on *Good Morning America* or David Letterman or something. That way Arthur will actually appear in her own collection."

At the mention of this, Arthur looked up from her writing and smiled. It was a nice smile. By the way, Arthur nearly always wears the same clothes every day, even though everyone teases her about it. It's because she won't buy girls' clothes and her mother refuses to shop in the boys' department for her. So she is stuck with one boy outfit that another GWAB member gave her out of pity—the red polo shirt and chinos.

"What's her collection?" I asked.

"Arthur collects *Retro TV Magazines,*" Jeremy explained.

"What's that?" I asked.

"They give the TV listings, just like *TV Guide,*" Jeremy said, "but they pay the most attention to the retro shows. You know, plot summaries, trivia, stuff like that. Arthur's had been collecting them since—how long, Arthur?"

"Since I was six."

"Really?" I said. That was actually impressive.

Weird, but impressive.

I left them to their work, and went to my room and sat down heavily on the edge of my bed. I usually went right to work on Nemesis, but the day had taken a toll on me. I felt completely unmotivated. And it was all because of Mason Ragg. Who, I now reminded myself, would be eating my three Oreo cookies tomorrow unless I found a way to prevent it.

That got me to my feet.

I went to my desk, pulled out my yellow graph paper notebook and a mechanical pencil, and started to draw. At first it was really just crazy doodles—a huge guillotine hanging from the ceiling above my lunch sack, a dagger that shot out of my lunch sack the second someone touched it, stuff like that. I got it out of my system, then I really settled down to business.

Have you ever heard of Ockham's razor? It's a principle that says the simplest solution is always the best solution.

What I came up with was spectacularly simple.

Mason enjoyed eating my Oreos, so why not make eating my Oreos a lot less enjoyable?

I went to the bathroom and opened the little linen closet. Mom keeps all her oddball remedies on the top shelf: burdock tinctures, nettle capsules, tea tree oil. It took a while to sort through it all and find what I was looking for, but I did. It was shoved into the back corner. I think Mom was embarrassed that she had to use it, especially since it wasn't natural or organic and it didn't have any herbal junk in it.

Facial hair bleach.

It's for those little moustaches that women sometimes get. I once caught Mom with the stuff slathered across her upper lip. It's white and thick. Much like the middle of an Oreo cookie. I looked in the box. It even had its own little spatula to spread the cream with. How convenient. I shoved the box back to the corner of the cabinet. I'd be using it in the morning.

Obviously, I didn't need to make any blueprints for this idea. Back in my room, I shut my graph paper notebook and opened the desk drawer to put it away, but I hesitated before I shut the drawer. I stared down at it for a moment, considering. Then I pulled the entire drawer out of the desk and put it on the floor. In the shallow gap between the runners and the bottom of the desk there was a small rectangular piece of pale green paper. I pulled it out, took a breath, and flipped it over so I could read the single word written on it:

SLOB

I knew the handwriting so well—the neat, round curves, the slight hook on the top of the *L*. My right hand held the paper and my left hand pressed against my stomach. It's funny how things can hurt and feel good at the same time.

"Owen?"

Hurriedly, I put the paper back in its hiding place and slid the drawer over it.

"Yeah?"

The door opened and Mom walked in, carrying a plastic bag.

"Hey, good-lookin'. How are you feeling?"

"A lot better. I think the peppermint really helped."

"Did it? Wow." She always sounds surprised when someone tells her that one of her remedies actually worked. "Have you been able to eat anything?"

"I had a few Oreos," I said. I figured it was better to fess up than have her discover the near empty package of cookies tomorrow morning. "That was all I could keep down," I added.

I could see she didn't like that, but she was so happy I was feeling better and that my recovery was in part due to her peppermint remedy, she didn't make a stink. Like I said, I'm not beyond lying on occasion.

"I have something for you." She handed me the plastic bag. Inside was a box that said *Li'l Inventor*. It was a kit to put together this plastic robot dog.

"It says on the box that you can make it chase its tail," she said.

"Great. Thanks," I said.

She means well.

8

Don't you love it when things work out exactly as you planned?

Mason Ragg rose up suddenly from his chair at the English workstation at 10:37, asked for the hall pass, and left the room. When he came back, he looked unusually pleased. He must have taken the cookies and not eaten them yet. Good. I wanted to be in the lunchroom when he did.

This time, I felt no panic. I didn't even run out in the hall to check my lunch sack. I knew what I would find. Instead, I calmly worked away at the art workstation on a clay model of an Egyptian sarcophagus for global studies. Rachel Lowry even came over, and said, "Can I see that?"

"Sure."

She picked the sarcophagus up and turned it this way and that.

"Cool," she said and put it back down. Her fingerprints were on either side of the sarcophagus. I left them there.

It was a very excellent morning.

Then came gym class.

On the way down there, we passed Jeremy and Arthur and six other girls standing outside their classroom, looking angry and holding signs saying things like WE WILL NOT BE BULLIED! and GWAB RULES! and the ill-advised MR. SHACKLY SUCKS! All the girls had extremely short hair, except for Jeremy, and were dressed like boys. You wouldn't think that there is that much of a difference in boys' and girls' clothes these days, but when you see a girl dressed in boys' clothes, the difference is very clear. Boys' clothes are a lot less interesting than girls', for one. And also, they fit girls funny—baggy in some places and tight in others. Except for Arthur. Her red polo shirt and chinos fit her just fine. Also, the GWABs held themselves differently than other girls. They slumped more, I think.

Unfortunately, there were no network news cameras or famous anchorpeople, but Sybil Tushman was there with her camcorder. She has a daily video blog on her website called *The Universe According to Sybil*. It's usually just Sybil talking about her older sister and how much she hates her but she also does some news segments about our school. Lots of kids in our school watch it, believe it or not.

"Lesby-girls," hissed someone from my class.

The GWABs didn't even bat an eye over that one. It wasn't anything they hadn't heard before, and anyway, they clearly had more important things on their minds.

I caught Jeremy's eye as I passed, and she looked back at

me, her face full of utter defiance. If I didn't know that she was just a new member of GWAB, I would have guessed that she was the president. She has this leadership aura. She may not be supersmart, but if you stick her in a crowd of people, she just pops, like a zebra-striped jeep in a shopping-mall parking lot.

In gym class, Mr. Wooly had set up a balance beam and a trampoline in the front of the gym, and now he was laying down a line of mats in the back of the gym. Not good.

"So are you going to take my advice, Flapjack?" Andre asked me as I took my place on my spot.

"The fat excuse or the lawsuit?" I asked.

"Both."

"Nope."

"Neither?"

"That's right." I was in a fairly cocky mood this morning.

Mr. Wooly had finished with the mats and was on his way back up front when he actually came up to me and patted me on the shoulder in a friendly sort of way.

"Morning, Birnbaum," Wooly said.

"He's scared you're going to make trouble for him about the dog harness thing," Andre whispered when Wooly had passed.

Andre was probably right about that.

"Well, I won't," I said.

Andre shook his head. He interlaced his fingers, flipped them upside down, and flexed his wrists. "You know what your problem is, Flapjack?"

I growled. Quietly.

"You think life has to be hard." He smiled at me, one of his windsurfing-in-Malibu smiles. I wanted to punch him right then and there, but suddenly his smile crumpled and he looked uneasy. I don't think I've ever seen him look like that before. He was looking at something behind me, so I turned my head to follow his gaze. Mason had come in the side door of the gym, accompanied by a teacher's aide. Up to now, I had mercifully been spared Mason's presence in gym class. Andre had told me that Mason had a "psycho exemption," although I assumed there was a more official word for it.

The teacher's aide went up to Mr. Wooly and began to talk to him with her back turned to the class in order to be discreet, but Mr. Wooly's face was clearly visible to all of us. And he was not happy. In fact, he made no effort to keep his voice down when he said, "Well, just so's we understand each other, I won't be held responsible when all hell breaks loose in here." The gym was dead quiet and his voice echoed so we all heard his words quite clearly. It was the first time all the rumors about Mason had been confirmed by an adult in the school.

The teacher's aide was now angry too. She pointed a finger at him and said, "That was massively inappropriate,

Gene." She didn't bother to keep her voice down either, so that we all heard her scolding him but more importantly, we caught that his name was Gene.

"Gene?!" Someone in our class repeated loudly in an incredulous voice.

"Settle down, people!" he called out to all of us. He probably would have called us "ladies" instead of "people" if the aide hadn't been there.

I was watching Mason. He had been working his jaw for several seconds, his mean little eyes fixed on Mr. Wooly. I suspected he was busy collecting a large glob of phlegm to use as a projectile.

Yeah, do it, Mason, I thought. Hit Mr. Wooly right in the face with a fat, juicy goober.

Instant revenge on both my enemies. You can see how much that would appeal to me, I'm sure.

"Mr. Ragg," Mr. Wooly said to Mason, "A4."

Mason's jaw stopped churning. He stood there for a moment, glaring at Mr. Wooly, until the aide put a careful hand on his back and guided him to the spot on the slickery gym floor, showing him the *A* on the wall to his right and the *4* on the wall behind Mr. Wooly.

Mason was front and center, directly in Mr. Wooly's line of fire.

Excellent.

During our stretches, Mr. Wooly made us do a tricky series of leg hops, which he'd never had us do before. There was a lot of "left, left, right, left, right, right," so that we had to keep switching legs in this random jig. We were all stumbling around—even Andre managed to look awkward. But today, Mason was Mr. Wooly's prime target.

"Keep up, Mr. Ragg!" Mr. Wooly shouted over the sound of furiously pounding sneakers. "This train doesn't stop for latecomers! It's sink or swim, pal! I see your feet moving, but the parade is passing you by!"

That's three mixed metaphors in a row, in case you didn't notice. Obviously, Mr. Wooly didn't.

I guess I should have felt pretty pleased that he was picking on Mason, but I couldn't somehow. Maybe it was because Mason's evil genius face was turned away from me. From my vantage point, all I could see was a kid with fast, skinny legs, hopping around really nimbly. You had to admire it somehow. It reminded me of some of those old cowboy movies, when the bad guy shoots at the feet of the good guy, which makes him dance around to avoid the bullets.

But Mason *was* the bad guy.

Still, at that moment, I admired him anyway.

Finally, Mr. Wooly called a stop to the idiotic warm-up and said it was time for gymnastics. I felt my stomach twist up.

"Today, my friends," Mr. Wooly announced, "we are going to engage in a little healthy competition."

Oh, blithering carbuncles.

I didn't really think that, you understand. I thought something else entirely, but it's not printable.

"I'll be separating you out into teams and we'll have a little gymnastic triathlon."

From his back pocket, he whipped out a list of all our names and which teams we were on. I tell you, he must have sweated over the thing all night long. For a subhuman bozo, Mr. Wooly could be diabolically clever when he wanted to be. The three teams were set up thusly:

1. Team A had one kid who was a superstar athlete (that was Andre) and a few other passably athletic kids
2. Team B had several wannabe superstar athletes who were clawing their way to the top and full of pent-up frustration that they were not the real, actual superstar athlete. They also had a few so-so-ish to poor athletes and one bully magnet whose job was to bring down the entire team. That would be me.

The combination was designed to not only foster competition between the teams, but also *within* the teams. Have you ever seen those movies about the Roman gladiator fights, where they tossed a bunch of poor guys into an arena with tigers and crocodiles?

Yeah.

That's right.

And I didn't even have a helmet or those nifty sandals.

But Mr. Wooly had another decision to make. He hadn't counted on Mason being there. After all the rest of us were herded into opposite ends of the gym, Mr. Wooly looked down at his list, then looked at Mason, who was still standing on A4. You could practically hear Mr. Wooly's Neanderthal brain whirring, trying to figure out where Mason would cause the most pain and suffering.

"Team B," Mr. Wooly finally said.

Of course.

Mason strutted over to our team, his chin tipped up, eyeing all of us. Clearly he was not going to disappoint Mr. Wooly. He stood a little apart from the rest of us, but to be honest, we were all standing apart from each other. No one on Team B seemed to want to be on Team B. Even I looked longingly at Team A where Andre was already having a sportsmanly chat with his team.

"This is so unfair," muttered a tall, pimply kid on our team named Jay, one of the Andre wannabes. "Andre gets Ron and Corey and Tristan, while Wooly gives us . . . what? A fat slob and a psycho."

Everyone on the team glanced at Mason nervously to see how he would react to that. No one looked at me nervously, of course, but I didn't expect them to.

Mason didn't say anything. He slowly reached down for his sock. All eyes followed his hand. We all saw it. The outline of something stuffed in his sock. Something distinctly knife-shaped. Eyes grew wide. Then Mason calmly tugged at the edge of his sock, just as though he was adjusting it to make all the lines in the cuff straight. He stood upright again, folded his arms against his chest, and quickly looked at all his teammates, as if daring them to say anything. None of them did.

So he *did* keep his famous switchblade in his sock. I'd have to tell Izzy.

Mason's little exhibition did one good thing at least. It stopped Team B's grumbling. All of a sudden, losing a gymnastic competition seemed somewhat less important than losing a thumb.

Mr. Wooly explained the triathlon's events course, which involved walking across the balance beam, jumping on the trampoline and tucking your legs, running a lap around the gym, then ending with a somersault on the mat.

That's *four* events, by the way. A triathlon would be *three* events, Mr. Wooly. That's *tri*-athalon. Never mind.

The teams would go one at a time, and he'd be timing them with a stopwatch. It would be relay race style, with points taken off if people botched the individual events. I could feel my teammates' eyes on me, Owen Birnbaum, The Imperial Botch-meister.

Team A was first. Mr. Wooly gave them a few minutes to figure out the lineup. Andre, of course, was the one who gave the orders, huddle style, arms over shoulders. It looked very professional. Our team was watching Team A enviously. There was no way we would get into a huddle. We didn't even want to be on the same side of the gym with each other, much less nose to nose. Team A unhuddled, Andre clapped a few times to get everyone pumped up, and they sent their first teammate out on the course.

I watched the first few guys pretty carefully to see how this thing was supposed to be done and to figure out just how badly I was going to embarrass myself and infuriate my teammates.

It was going to be ugly.

Mr. Wooly stood at the finish line with his thumb poised over his stopwatch. All the members of Team A finished their course. A few kids missed the leg tuck on the trampoline and five of them fell off the beam, but all in all, they did pretty well. Andre, of course, did it all so effortlessly that for a moment I wondered if he was one of those undercover cops they send into schools to masquerade as schoolchildren.

One of the kids on my team groaned and said, "We might actually stand a chance if we didn't have blubber butt on our team."

I felt my teammates' eyes turn on me bitterly. I didn't look back at them, yet I couldn't help but catch Mason's face in my peripheral vision, staring at me. Not with resentment, but with curiosity.

Ah, yes, I thought. He's never witnessed Owen Birnbaum in gym class before. Well, this will be a rare treat for him.

Mr. Wooly turned to our team. His face was a little too animated, too interested. You could see he was thinking, Okay, Gene, now the fun begins.

"Team B!" he barked. "Figure out your lineup."

We didn't have Andre to take charge. Instead, we had five wannabe-but-never-will-be Andres who all wanted to take charge. After a brief "discussion," a full-out shoving match broke out between three of those guys. Mr. Wooly stepped in quickly and stopped it, but you could tell he was already well satisfied because he kept wiping his hand over the lower half of his face, as if in exasperation. But if you really looked, you could make out a smile that he was trying to cover. *I* was really looking.

And he noticed I was really looking.

The guilt/fear that he appeared to be feeling earlier vanished. He didn't need to cover the lower half of his face anymore. The smile was gone.

He walked right up to me and said, "Mr. Birnbaum. You're a smart boy, aren't you?"

I didn't quite know how to answer that.

I didn't need to, as it turned out, since Mason answered it for me.

He snorted.

I whipped around to stare at him.

Mason's horrible face was perfectly calm, his eyes meeting mine evenly.

"Well, well!" Mr. Wooly said jovially. He was enjoying this unexpected turn. "So you have a little competition in the brain department, Birnbaum? Well, that's okay. Two heads are better than one, eh? All right, since Birnbaum and Ragg are the smart ones on Team B, they'll decide the lineup together. And remember"—he pointed a finger at

Mason and me—"the lineup can make or break the success of your team."

There were explosions of fury at this decree from the wannabes, but Mr. Wooly made them shut up then left us to our task. Now pretty much everyone on Team B was glaring at us.

"Okay," I said as confidently as I could manage, "here's the lineup." I listed off a bunch of names. It was completely random, except for the fact that I went first. I had already figured out that if I went in the beginning, my other teammates would be too nervous about their upcoming turns to pay as much attention to me. If I went at the end, everyone would be relaxed enough to laugh their heads off.

"Wrong," Mason said.

"What's wrong about it?" I asked. The other kids on Team B were pretty riveted by now. The fat slob and the psycho were going to have it out.

"You should be last and I should be second to last."

"Forget it," I said, folding my arms across my chest. It's not something I do often, and I was sorry I did it now. It makes me look like the Buddha in Nima's living room. And yes, I was aware that I was arguing with a kid who kept a knife in his sock, but you have never seen me on a trampoline.

"Clock's ticking! Five, four, three—" Mr. Wooly shouted at us.

Mason spit out another lineup, again putting me last and him second to last.

"Two one. Okay, Team B. Step up."

Everyone hustled toward the equipment, arranging themselves in Mason's sequence.

"No!" I said again, but Mason shoved by me and said, "Shut up."

Mr. Wooly blew his whistle, and Steve Taylor shot off toward the balance beam. So that was that. I was doomed. I would be the last one. The grand finale. I'd be flopping all over the gym and everyone would be screaming with laughter, thanks to Mason.

No, Team A would be screaming with laughter. Team B would be screaming with rage.

The first couple of guys did really well, which made me feel like vomiting. None of them even toppled off the balance beam. Now we were actually contenders for the winning spot, which made my situation increasingly worse. In fact, it all might come down to me in the end. I glared at Mason. Look, I'm used to bullies. I was never exactly popular, even before I was fat. Back then I was picked on because I was smart. When I started gaining all this weight, about a year and half ago (I gained it so fast and so furiously that I have stretch marks across my thighs and belly), I became the person everyone loves to hate.

Still, most of the kids who picked on me were morons. Yes, the things they said and did hurt my feelings, but they were thoughtless insults from teeny-tiny minds.

Mason Ragg, however, seemed to be thinking.

Darren Rosenberg was finishing up on the mats, and

Mason stepped up to the starting line. His jaw was working again. I was beginning to think this wasn't a sign that he was going to spit at someone, but instead it was a sign of nervousness. Darren tagged him on his shoulder—carefully, I noticed—and Mason headed for the balance beam. The strange thing was, though, he didn't run to it, like everyone else. He just walked. Actually, it was more of an amble. Team B started shouting at him, "Run, run!! What are you doing?"

I had fairly good idea about what he was doing. He was trying to make it even harder on me. Team B would be so behind on time that the pressure would be on me to make it up.

When he got to the balance beam, he eased himself up and inch by inch made his way across. Shuffle, shuffle, shuffle. As though he were terrified of heights. Well, maybe he is, I thought. He certainly looked scared.

Team B was practically rabid. "Go!" they screamed. "Can you freaking believe this?" And other choice things.

When he was halfway across the beam, the fire drill sounded.

There was a cry of outrage from Team A and a cry of joy from Team B and a cry of "Shut it!" from Mr. Wooly. While everyone else was hustling out of the gym or appealing to Mr. Wooly for a rematch, Mason got off the balance beam. I watched him. He had no trouble with balance. He had no issues with height. He had hopped off the beam and landed on the floor mat as easily as a cat.

He was diabolical.

Our eyes met, and he smiled at me. This was a definite smile. A gloating smile that crinkled up his scar.

Do you know what I did then? I actually smiled back. And this is the weird part. I don't know how to explain it. For a split second, I felt like Mason and I were on the same side rather than sworn enemies. Amazing what a smile can do to you physiologically. I think it pumps up the endorphins so you automatically feel like the universe is a good and friendly place.

That lasted all of twelve minutes.

Nine minutes of standing outside in the frigid cold in my gym shorts, two and half minutes of walking to the lunch closet. At the twelfth minute, I discovered that my entire lunch sack was gone.

In its place was a note. It said:

NEXT TIME I LEAVE THE CLASS, COUNT TO 20, THEN FOLLOW ME.

9

"I wouldn't," said Izzy. He had given me half his sandwich since I didn't have anything to eat at lunch. "It's probably a trick. He'll get you into some dark corner and pull out his buck knife."

"Switchblade. And it *is* in his sock," I said. My voice was dead-sounding. "By the way."

"Oh, dude." Izzy shook his head, looking at me piteously.

Mason was sitting at a corner table in the lunchroom, all by himself as usual. There was no sign of my lunch sack anywhere around him. He'd probably taken out its contents and dumped the bag. Mom would not be happy. She hated wastefulness. Plus, she'd ask how it had happened and I would have to make up a lie.

Every so often I glanced over to see if Mason was eating my cookies yet. Seeing Mason gag on facial hair bleach cream was the only glimmer of possible satisfaction in this whole situation. The lunch bell rang and Mason got up and dumped the contents of his tray in the trash. He hadn't eaten any Oreos as far as I could tell.

"Just think," Izzy said, "anything could happen over the weekend. Mason might get run over by a truck."

"Or he might devise a new and improved way to torment me."

"Think positive, man, think positive."

I spent most of Friday afternoon at the Ninety-third Street demo site alone (Jeremy was busy plotting out some new GWAB scheme with Arthur) poking through the same debris in the hopes that I'd find an amplifier. I didn't find one. In fact, there wasn't much of anything left at that site. The only thing I took was a plastic bag full of small metal brackets.

On my way home, I saw a group of kids hanging out together on the steps of a brownstone. I crossed to the other side of the street. A group of kids hanging out always spells trouble for me. But to my surprise, the kids were actually calling to me. Not by name, but a few of them were waving their arms for me to come over.

I'm not a moron. I ignored them. But when they quieted down I glanced over. The steps of the brownstone were strewn with stuff—toys, games, lamps, books. Stuff. It's really hard for me to turn my back on stuff. So I crossed the street.

The kids spotted me crossing and immediately started

frantically motioning for me to come over again. I was guessing that sales hadn't been stellar.

"Anything on the first three steps is one dollar," a girl explained to me. "Everything above that is two dollars."

"But we're willing to negotiate," a boy added. He was a little chunky. Not fat like me, but he was younger too. I had a sudden urge to warn him. Life is tough when you are significantly fatter than the national average, kid. You might want to cut back on the Cheez Doodles.

But who am I to give advice?

After a quick scan of all their items, I could see there was nothing I wanted. "Sorry," I said, and started to leave.

"But we have a large selection of board games," the chunky boy said, sweeping his arm across a stack of beat-up board game boxes.

"Thanks, but I don't need any," I said, backing away.

"Well, what *do* you need?" the boy persisted. He was a natural salesman, actually. You had to admire that. So I played along.

"I need a forty-decibel amplifier." I smiled as I said it. It reminded me of playing bank teller with Jeremy when we were little kids—"I'd like to withdraw fifty billion dollars, please." "Here you go, ma'am. Don't spend it all in one place."

But this kid, he wasn't playing around.

"Hold on," he said, jabbing a finger at me. "I think I may have what you need."

He jumped up and ran inside the brownstone. He was gone for a good five minutes, during which the other kids tried to convince me that I needed a pair of binoculars with one busted lens.

Finally the brownstone door opened and the kid came out with this huge smile on his face, carrying a rectangular black metal box. He walked down the steps and thrust the black box toward me.

"Is this was you're looking for?" he asked.

You know what? It was.

"Two dollars," he said.

Once again, I'm not a moron. I knew this didn't come from the bottom of the kid's toy chest.

"Okay, who does this belong to?" I asked him. I tried to use my stern voice.

"Don't worry, don't worry." The kid waved a casual hand in the air. I'm telling you, he was a pro. "It used to belong to my older brother, but he got a new one and this is just sitting around in the back of his closet."

It might have been the truth, who knows. That's what I told myself as I dug through my backpack and collected up the spare coins that were floating around in there. Altogether I had one dollar and sixty-three cents.

"Sold!" the boy said and pocketed my change hurriedly. I suspect he was worried that his older brother would come home any minute.

At the apartment I hooked up the amplifier. It took

some time. Jeremy came in and when I told her about it, she said, "That's it, then! Nemesis will work!"

"Don't get all excited yet," I warned her. "Even if we can get a strong signal, there's another problem."

It was a doozy too. I had thought about it long and hard but couldn't figure out how to solve it.

"We're looking for a specific day two years ago, right?" I said.

Jeremy nodded. "October 25."

"Right," I said. It bothered me that the date flew right off her tongue so easily. It was hard for me to say that date without my voice sounding weird. "So, even if I do manage to pick up a signal from the past, I have to be able to figure out when that signal was first sent out."

"Oh." She sounded so disappointed. It reminded me that if this project worked, it was going to affect both of us, not just me.

"I'll figure it out," I assured her.

I sounded more confident than I felt. I had no idea how I was going to figure it out. I mulled over the problem as I worked. I mulled it over as I ate dinner. And I mulled it over some more that night as I went back to work on the amplifier. But I was getting no closer to a solution. I was just getting more and more frustrated. To take my mind off it, I turned on the TV and watched some really stupid sitcoms, but they were so stupid that my mind drifted back to the problem. I guess I can't stop myself from thinking for very long. As it turned out, though, the solution was staring me right in my face.

The TV.

I jumped up and ran to Jeremy's room. Jeremy was already in bed when I knocked on her door. She sleeps with her head under her blanket. She always has. It used to make me crazy when she was really little. I was convinced she would suffocate, or at the very least suffer irreparable brain damage from lack of oxygen, so I would slip into her room every night and pull her blanket off her head. By the morning it was always back over her head again, and eventually I gave up.

I sat on her bed and said her name a few times but she didn't respond. I've never seen anyone sleep as heavily as Jeremy sleeps. You almost have to get rough with her in order to wake her. I pushed her shoulder a few times. When that didn't work, I pulled the covers off her head and pinched her cheek.

That worked.

"Hey!" She sat up like a shot, her hair wild.

"Listen," I said, "do you think Arthur would let me borrow her old *Retro TV Magazines*?"

"That's why you woke me up?" She collapsed back down on the mattress and pulled the covers over her head.

"This is important, Jeremy. What do you think?"

She didn't have to think very long. She answered instantly, "No, I'm absolutely positive that she wouldn't."

"Why not?"

"Because she's very protective of her collection." Her voice was muffled under the blanket. "She keeps them all in individual plastic sleeves, and she puts on these white gloves when she reads them."

"That is really weird, you know."

There was a pause during which I guessed she was trying to think of a way to defend Arthur. But she couldn't, so she said, "Yeah, I know."

"Will you ask her anyway?" I said. "This is really important."

"What's so important about old *Retro TV Magazines*?" she asked. She took the blanket off her head to look at me.

I told her all about my new idea. She listened carefully. She doesn't usually understand the stuff I explain to her, but she always listens carefully. I told her that if I could pull in some television signals from two years ago, I could check the old TV guides and figure out the date when those shows were first being aired. That way I could put a date on the old signals.

"That's so cool," she said. "Yeah. That might totally work."

She sounded so optimistic, which I appreciated. I know people would say it's just because she didn't understand how difficult this thing was and how slim the odds were that it would work. But I didn't care. It boosted my confidence to hear the faith in her voice.

"All right," she said. "I'm seeing Arthur tomorrow anyway. We're working on the official GWAB statement to be read at The Blue and White Rebellion. I'll ask her about the television guides then."

I thought about asking what The Blue and White Rebellion was, but I decided I probably didn't want to know.

"Later," Jeremy said, "I'm going to attempt to teach her how to skate backwards, although she's still a little shaky on the forwards part. She has really weak ankles. You wouldn't think it from looking at her, would you?"

The next day, Jeremy called me from Arthur's house.

The answer was no.

To be exact, it was, "You must be kidding! He couldn't pay me enough to borrow my collection!"

"She won't budge either," Jeremy said. "I've tried."

I had been expecting this.

"Let me talk to her," I said.

"It's not going to help," Jeremy said. In a whisper, she added, "Actual spit flew out of her mouth when she said '*pay*.'"

"Just let me try."

There was a pause during which I could hear the muffled arguments between the two of them. Finally, there was a scraping noise and Arthur's sullen voice came on.

"Yeah?" she said.

"Arthur, I think we can make a deal," I said.

"No."

"Just listen. In the back of my closet I have a bag that is stuffed full of clothes. Boys' clothes."

There was a hesitation. "*Your* clothes, you mean?" she asked.

"From two years ago."

Again a pause. "Look, I don't want to be mean or anything, but I really don't think I would fit into your clothes."

"I wasn't fat two years ago," I said. "I was like you. Not fat, not thin. If you don't believe me, ask Jeremy."

She did. She clanked the phone down immediately. There was some discussion. Mostly I could hear Jeremy's ardent voice. She was probably listing all the choice boy clothes in the bag. I know she went through the bag herself when she first joined GWAB, but she's such a small, skinny kid that she was swimming in my old stuff. Arthur, on the other hand, would fit into them perfectly.

"She says okay." It was Jeremy on the line now.

"Great."

"But there are rules. She'll lend the collection to you for two weeks, that's it. You have to keep them in order, and you have to wear gloves when you handle them."

I heard Arthur's voice in the background, and Jeremy added, "She says she will know if you haven't worn the gloves."

I briefly had an image of her dusting the *Retro TV Magazines* for fingerprints.

"Not a problem," I said.

"All right. You can bring the clothes to Arthur's house now and we'll make the switch."

It was all very dramatic, as you can see. I didn't mind, though, because it felt dramatic to me too.

This might be it, I kept thinking. A hundred years from now, people would still be talking about the Birnbaum *Retro TV Magazine* Theory, the way they talk about Newton's apple.

I went into my closet and dug through all the crap that had accumulated over the past two years—salvaged items that I knew I'd never use and old school notebooks. Way in the back was a black Hefty bag. I dragged it out, tearing the bag in the process. If I hadn't had to transfer all the clothes to an old duffel bag, I probably wouldn't have looked at them. I held them up, one by one. Had my body once fit into these things? It was almost unimaginable. I felt like I must have been a totally different person. Like I had died and been reborn as someone else. I remembered things I had forgotten about too, the way you do when you look at old photographs. I could remember that I had worn one particular shirt on our trip to Ottawa, or how my NY Yankees shirt always made my parents squabble about baseball teams—my mother was from Boston.

After all the clothes were in the duffel bag, I zipped it up. Done, I thought. I've seen them, and I won't ever have to see them again.

I couldn't figure out if that made me happy or sad.

I took the bus to Arthur's house because the duffel bag was too heavy to carry the whole way if I walked. She lived on the fifth floor of an old walk-up apartment building, and the duffel bag wasn't light, so by the time I pushed the doorbell, I was huffing and puffing and sweating like a hog.

Arthur's mother answered the door. She looked perplexed for a moment to see a kid she didn't know holding a duffel bag, like I was coming to stay for a few weeks. Thankfully, Jeremy and Arthur had hurried up behind her, dragged me into Arthur's room, and closed the door.

I looked around the room in amazement. Without Arthur, eBay probably would collapse.

The entire room was decorated with retro television paraphernalia. Her walls were covered with posters of *Charlie's Angels, Gilligan's Island, The Brady Bunch,* plus a bunch of other shows I'd never heard of. There was a special section by her bed devoted entirely to some greasy-haired guy in a leather jacket. She had a bookshelf without any books. Instead the shelves were crammed with retro TV lunch boxes and action figures.

In every direction you looked there was something retro TV. Even up. A cheesy paper mobile hung from a thumbtack in the ceiling with photos of the leather jacket guy dangling from wires.

The *Retro TV Magazines*, however, were nowhere in sight.

I felt a tug at my duffel bag.

"Is this them?" Arthur asked. She looked practically feverish, she was so excited.

"Yes," I said, tightening my grip on the bag. "Where are the *Retro TV Magazines*?"

"Oh. Okay." She said this like she was disappointed I had remembered the bargain. She went to her dresser and pulled open the drawers, one by one, six drawers all together.

Holy cannoli.

The *Retro TV Magazine*s were there, pressed together in their little plastic bags. No clothes. Just *Retro TV Magazines*. She had even made dividers to separate the years.

"Wow." I said.

"I told you," Jeremy said.

I started to walk toward the dresser, but Arthur quickly turned around with her arms spread protectively in front of the drawers. She went over the rules again. I agreed again. Still, she hesitated.

"How about he swears on *Him?*" Jeremy suggested.

"Good idea," Arthur said.

"Who's *Him?*" I asked. I looked around the room for a shrine, like Nima has. The entire room was a shrine.

Arthur went to her bookshelf and picked up a little action figure. A greasy-haired man in a leather jacket, with his hands shaped in a thumbs-up position. It was the guy on the mobile.

"Arthur Fonzarelli. The Fonz," Jeremy explained. "He's on this old TV show *Happy Days*. She worships him."

"Oh, got it." So I held The Fonz in my left hand, put my right hand over my heart, and solemnly swore that I would take excellent care of the *Retro TV Magazine*s and would always remember to wear the gloves.

That seemed to do the trick.

She packed them up. I only needed the ones from the past two years, and the most current one—which she hated to part with, but did—so they actually fit into a single carton. She also put a pair of white gloves in the box and gave me a meaningful look.

Jeremy helped me home with the carton, and I spent the rest of the afternoon looking at lists of TV shows, deciding what television channel to zero in on. And yes, I wore the white gloves. The nature of *Retro TV Magazine* narrowed down my options quite a bit. It was like the people who wrote this thing were still living in the 1970s. Sure, it listed the names of the people who would appear on the late-night talk shows and it gave very brief descriptions of what you could expect to see on the new shows. But when it came to the old reruns, it gave these long, detailed descriptions of the episodes. Like "*The Love Boat*, Episode Title: 'Ex Plus Y.' A divorced couple take the cruise with their new partners and keep bumping into their exes. Does all their bickering mean that they are still really in love? Also, two teens are caught in a budding romance while some feisty senior citizens threaten to mess up Julie's new romance. Trivia Question: What *Happy Days* heartthrob plays one of the teens?"

And on and on. It was pretty ridiculous. But I needed to

have detailed descriptions of the old shows to figure out when they were aired and pinpoint the time that the star Nemesis was bouncing back the radio waves.

Jeremy came in, sat down on my bed, and watched me for a little bit.

"Hungry?" she asked. "Mom left us some casserole thing."

Mom always worked late on Saturday, so for dinner we had to fend for ourselves.

"Not really," I said with my nose tucked into the *Retro TV Magazine*s.

"*Really?*" She looked at me so strangely, which made me realize it *was* strange that I wasn't hungry.

"Have you figured out which channel you're going to tune to?" she asked.

I just had. "The Freakout Channel. It's all seventies shows, all the time."

"Okay." Jeremy clapped once. "Now we have the right channel. What do we do next?"

She enjoyed feeling like she was a part of Nemesis. And she was, in a way. She scavenged a lot of the materials for Nemesis, so I felt it was only fair to let her help a little.

I let her help me set up some of the equipment and explained to her that we were only testing things out at this point. That we would probably get no results whatsoever, and that was normal. There were lots of adjustments that still had to be made.

"Oh, yeah, sure," she said breezily. I really don't think she understood.

I tuned the TV to channel 74, which is the Freakout Channel. We don't get that channel on our regular TV, but with luck it would come through with the help of Nemesis, just like the farm channel did. Only a whole lot clearer.

Nothing happened. I adjusted the satellite dish for a few minutes, hoping, hoping . . . The sound came through first, then the picture. Yes! It was the Freakout Channel. The picture was far from perfect, but it was clear enough. We sat there on the bed, watching this show called *Mork and Mindy,* which funnily enough was about a guy from outer space. He lands on earth and moves into the attic of this cute girl's place. I watched enough of it to get the gist of the episode then checked the most current *Retro TV Magazine* for today's listing. There it was. The very same episode. Okay, I admit there was a part of me that was hoping we'd pick up a two-year-old signal right off the bat. But the sensible part of me knew that it probably wouldn't happen that easily. It was lucky that we'd been able to pick up the Freakout Channel at all.

After *Mork and Mindy*, we watched an episode of *Sanford and Son*, then *The Love Boat,* then two back-to-back episodes of *Gilligan's Island,* then *I Dream of Jeannie.* After a while I felt Jeremy's eyes on me.

"What?" I said, keeping my eyes on the screen. If we caught some two-year-old signals, it might be only a second-long glimpse of the "wrong" show and I didn't want to miss it.

"Maybe we should call it quits for the night," Jeremy said.

My eyes left the screen. She was right. I think I had been temporarily hypnotized by hope and a blond genie in a pink harem outfit.

10

There wasn't much time to work with Nemesis on Sunday. Sunday is Family Day. Mom always digs through the newspapers to find something "interesting" for us to do together. It's pretty hit or miss. That Sunday it was miss.

She said she was taking us to a puppet show, which we objected to immediately.

"In case you haven't noticed, we're not five years old, Zelda," Jeremy said.

I watched Mom press her lips together and blink a little too quickly when Jeremy called her Zelda. Mom hears the most hair-raising things every day and she has to always keep her cool, but I could see how much it bugged her every time Jeremy called her Zelda. Of course, so could Jeremy, which is why she did it. Still, Mom is stubborn too, so she said, "It's not a kids' puppet show, Caitlin. It's supposed to be very sophisticated."

Grrrr. That was approximately the sound that came out

of Jeremy's mouth. Unlike Mom, she has no training in keeping her cool.

Mom was right in the end. It was not a kids' puppet show. It was about this lady puppet that has loads of boyfriend puppets, and after about fifteen minutes, most of the puppets had no clothes on. Mom made us all stand up and leave.

"Sorry about that, guys," Mom said when we were outside the theater. I wasn't sorry I'd seen it though. It was kind of fascinating in an embarrassing sort of way, but when Jeremy whispered that one of the boyfriend puppets reminded her of Andre, I was glad we'd left when we did.

To make up for it, Mom bought tickets for us to take the Circle Line, a boat that sails around the island of Manhattan. It was a very touristy thing to do, which means it was also expensive. Normally Mom would have said that we couldn't afford it, but maybe she thought the bracing watery breezes would purify our brains of the puppet show contamination.

It worked in a way. Ten minutes after the boat set sail, I forgot all about the naked puppets and all I could think about was *Gilligan's Island*. It was one of the shows I was watching on the Freakout Channel. In case you don't know it, it's this show where these people get stranded on a desert island and are always trying to find a way to escape. But they've made the island pretty comfortable with these nice huts and they put on plays and have golfing competitions and turtle races, which makes you wonder if the reason they never escape is because they don't really want to.

Manhattan is an island. Of course, everyone knows that, but it's so smooshed with buildings and people and police sirens and street fairs and restaurants that it's easy to forget it. You think it's the center of the universe when you're in it. From the boat, though, you can't believe how puny it all is.

"Weird," Mom said in this dreamy kind of voice.

"Yeah," both Jeremy and I said at the same time. We all understood each other. All three of us were outside on deck even though it was cold. The wind was making us all squint, and Jeremy's hair was flying every which way.

"Our mother and father took us on the Circle Line one time," Jeremy said.

I sucked in my breath. There was a moment of silence during which I was grateful that I had the island of Manhattan to focus on while waiting for someone to say the right thing. I was pretty sure that it wouldn't be me.

"I bet they had more sense than to take you on it in frickin' arctic weather," Mom said.

That was the right thing to say.

We laughed, not the least because we'd never heard Mom say "frickin'" before.

"No, it was summer," Jeremy said. "And remember that kid on the bridge?" she said to me.

I nodded, actually surprised that I did remember.

"What about the kid on the bridge?" Mom asked. She

was half smiling at us, as though this just was an everyday conversation rather than the first time we had all spoken about my parents since we came to live with Mom.

"The kid was standing on one of the bridges, and right before the boat went under the bridge, he pulled down his pants and mooned us," I told her.

"And remember what Dad did?" Jeremy said. "He laughed so hard that Coke shot out of his nose, and that made Mom laugh so hard that she started snorting. Remember how she snorted when she laughed hard?"

We stayed out on deck the whole trip, even when everybody else went inside the cabin. By the time we reached the pier, my fingers were stiff with cold and Jeremy's face was as red as a radish, but I think I can safely say that we all went home feeling better about everything than we had in a long time.

After an early dinner I went into my room and right away turned on Nemesis. All that talk about my parents made me more determined than ever. Their faces appeared so clearly in my mind—my dad's black moustache that twitched when he was about to say something funny. The kind green eyes that always had tired pouches beneath them. My mother's eyes were also green, but a different green from Dad's. So light they were almost the color of ginger ale. Sometimes she watched Jeremy and me so intensely, it was like she was wondering what we were going to be like when we grew up, and I always had the urge to tell her not to worry, we'd be fine. I really wish I had.

I turned on the TV and waited. I reasoned that if I did manage to catch an old signal, there would be a sudden change in the quality of the picture—more staticky, just like in the "ghost" images at The Black Baron Pub. And then, of course, the show would be different than the one I had been watching.

I watched an episode of *Happy Days*.

Nothing happened.

Then I watched an episode of *The Beverly Hillbillies*.

Nothing happened. I was beginning to think that I might need a low-noise amplifier to make my signal stronger. But those things were pricey, and the odds of finding one at a demo site would be pretty slim. Or maybe a bigger satellite dish would do the trick . . .

Or maybe you're kidding yourself that this could ever work in a hundred billion years, I heard my brain grumble.

Shut up, I told myself. All the great inventors have had moments of doubt. Thomas Edison once said, "I have not failed. I've just found ten thousand ways that won't work."

I watched an episode of *The Brady Bunch*, during which I decided I liked Jan better than Marcia because she reminded me of Rachel Lowry except with long hair and braces. Rachel's teeth are really nice, by the way.

There was a knock on the door and Mom poked her head in.

"Hey, good lookin'. Any idea where your lunch sack is?" she said.

Oops.

"I think . . . oh. Sack, hmm. I left it at school," I said.

Can you tell I'm not a good liar?

Mom listens to people on the phone all day long, liars included. I'm sure she knew I was lying.

"Everything okay at school?"

"Fine."

"Did someone take that lunch sack from you?" she asked.

Do you see what I mean about her?

"Yeah, but it's no big deal," I said.

"Stealing is a big deal," she said. "A very big deal." She was getting all worked up. Boy, you'd think someone who hears about people falling onto subway tracks and getting their arms sliced off or about people tossing their wives out a hotel window wouldn't care about a little thing like lunch sack theft.

"No, I know it is. It's okay. I know who did it. I'm going to get it back."

"Maybe I should have a talk with your teacher," she said.

"No! Let me handle this!" I don't generally raise my voice at her. Jeremy was at the door like a shot.

"What?" Jeremy said. "What's going on?"

"Someone stole your brother's lunch sack," Mom said.

I groaned. This was all getting way out of hand.

Jeremy frowned at me and folded her arms against her chest. "Do you know who?" she asked.

"No one you know," I said. The last thing I needed was for her to chase after Mason Ragg.

"All right, Owen." Mom backed down. "I'll let you handle this one." Maybe she didn't want to ruin our perfect day.

"Thanks."

"So," Mom said, glancing at the TV, "*The Brady Bunch*? I didn't know kids still watched that show."

"Some of us do."

"You probably think Marcia's cute, huh?" she said.

"Jan."

"Really?" She tipped her head to one side and smiled. I had the feeling that she was always the girl that never got any valentines.

"Yeah. Definitely Jan."

"All right, buddy. But next time someone is bullying you, will you promise me that you'll tell the teacher?"

I nodded.

I could feel Jeremy's eyes on me. I didn't like the way she was looking at me. It felt like she was *looking at me*. And that for the first time she was seeing me for who I really was.

That night I slept with the TV on. I just couldn't bring myself to turn it off, in case something happened.

Which it didn't.

11

"What's up, Flapjack?" Andre Bertoni jogged up to me and Jeremy on our way to school and he thumped me on my back.

Andre Bertoni is not someone you want to see first thing on Monday morning. There's way too much thumping.

Quickly, I crushed the I ♥ Puffins tote bag against my jacket. Mom had put my lunch in the tote bag, much to my horror, but I had rolled it up into a cylinder as best as I could to hide the huge puffin on the side.

"What you got there, Flapjack? Is that a puffin?"

"It wasn't *his* idea," Jeremy was quick to defend me. "Someone stole his usual lunch sack."

Then she turned bright red again because Andre Bertoni looked at her.

"Well, it wasn't me," Andre said, getting all bristly.

"No one said it was," I told him.

"Well, she's looking at me funny," he said, nodding at Jeremy, who then turned a shade redder. You'd think if you were all heartthrobby like Andre, you'd know when a girl is turning red because she's madly in love with you or because she thinks you stole her brother's lunch sack and wants to pulverize you.

"I already *know* who stole it," I reassured him.

"Really?" I could practically see his shoulder muscles relax. Frankly, if I didn't know who stole my lunch sack, I might have started to suspect Andre. "Who?"

"Mason Ragg," I said.

"Oh, man." Andre thumped me on the back of my neck. "That's who I wanted to talk to you about. Listen, don't mess with that lunatic. Did you know he carries a razor under his tongue?"

"A switchblade. In his sock."

"Here's the thing," Andre said. "I was at basketball practice on Friday, and I went to get a drink of water at the fountain. That's when I overheard my coach talking to Mr. Wooly about you."

"Me!?" I couldn't imagine the name Owen Birnbaum being tossed around the gymnasium on off-hours.

"You *and* Mason Ragg. Wooly thinks the two of you were up to something at the triathlon. He thinks you two knew that there was going to be a fire drill and that's why you arranged it so that you were both last."

"That's ridiculous! How would we know there was going to be a fire drill?" I said. "Besides, why would Mason and I be up to *anything* together? We can't stand each other!"

Andre shrugged. "All I know is that Wooly is planning something special for the two of you at the next gym class."

"What's he planning?" I'm not going to lie to you. I didn't ask this question with a nice, calm question mark at the end, like the one written here. I asked it with three exclamation points at the end, in bold letters, and underlined. In other words, I shrieked it.

Andre shrugged again. "I don't know. But if I were you, I'd reconsider getting that fat exemption ASAP." He thumped me on the belly.

"What's a fat exemption?" Jeremy asked when Andre was gone.

"Nothing," I grumbled.

"Owen?"

"What?"

"Maybe it's better that those Oreos get taken."

"What do you mean?" I asked.

"I mean maybe you shouldn't be eating Oreos at all, you know."

"No, I don't know. What do you mean?"

Of course I knew exactly what she meant. But never, NEVER had Jeremy said anything about my being fat. She was always the one who didn't care. She was always the one who never even seemed to notice, who saw me for who I was, underneath all the blubber.

"Why can't you at least try harder to lose weight, Owen? People make fun of you, you know. I've heard people laugh at you. They make you the butt of their jokes in front of everybody, even though they're friends, and I defend you, I do, but you could at least *try* to lose the weight. You weren't always fat."

She blurted this out as though it had been something she had been wanting to say for a long time.

There it was. Everything had changed in a minute between us. She no longer thought I was a better person than I actually was.

"Fine," I said to her, "if you're so embarrassed of me, walk to school by yourself." I ran ahead. I'm not an elegant runner, and once I started running I wished I hadn't because my jacket got caught in the back of my pants and I had to yank it back down over my rear end.

All morning long I fumed about my argument with Jeremy and worried about what Mr. Wooly was planning. Fuming, worrying, fuming, worrying. I clutched my clay sarcophagus so hard that I snapped off the tip of it while I was painting it. Rachel Lowry helped me glue it back on. That was nice. Her breath smelled like toothpaste and construction paper.

Ms. Bussle made Mason Ragg spend some time in the math workstation because she said his name hadn't appeared on the station's sign-up sheet at all last week. One of the math books was open in front of him, and from a distance it looked like he was writing diligently on a worksheet when in actuality he was drawing something on the desk.

At 10:57 he rose suddenly and walked up to Ms. Bussle's desk for the hall pass.

I'm not a spur-of-the-moment kind of guy, but my sister was disgusted with me, Wooly was planning to polish the gym floor with me, and it looked like the only thing Nemesis could do was pick up stupid seventies sitcoms. What did I have to lose, really? I stood up and went to Ms. Bussle's desk.

"Hall pass."

"Please," she said.

"Please."

She looked me over to see if it was once again something I had eaten. When she saw I looked fine, she handed me a hall pass.

I hadn't counted to twenty like the note suggested, but I was pretty sure it was close enough.

The hall directly outside the classroom was empty, but I could hear footsteps echoing down the hallway that joined it at a right angle. I walked quickly, thankful that I was wearing a pair of unsqueaky sneakers. As I passed the lunch closet, I quickly glanced at the shelf where I had put the I ♥ Puffins tote bag. It was still there, rolled up in a cylinder the way I had left it. He wouldn't have had time to rummage through it anyway. I turned down the adjoining hallway and could see Mason Ragg way up ahead. He was heading for the stairwell. I ducked behind a water fountain and peered out at him. The strange thing was that he never once turned to see if I was behind him. Maybe he didn't have to. Maybe he just knew that I would follow him, even when I didn't know it myself.

When I could just see the top of his head as he walked down the stairs, I started following again. I reached the staircase as he made the turn down the second flight of stairs.

That's when I remembered what Izzy said about Mason attacking me in a dark corner.

I froze, listening hard. I could hear footsteps, faint and apparently descending the stairs at a fast clip. If they were Mason's footsteps, he definitely wasn't waiting for me. On the contrary, it sounded like he was running. What on earth was he up to?

I hurried down the stairs. At this rate, I might easily lose track of him. I remembered how fast his legs moved in gym class. I hurried faster, already feeling the dampness of sweat in my armpits. Soon I'd be huffing.

I cleared the second staircase and went through the doors to the first floor. I looked around quickly. There were three hallways—one to my left, one to my right, and one dead ahead. Mason was hurrying along on the left.

He turned around suddenly, and my heart stopped cold. I thought for sure he would run at me, showering me with curses at the very least, at the very worst reaching for his sock. But instead, he did the oddest thing. He actually looked terrified. Then he turned around again and began to run like mad.

He skidded to a stop in front of one of the doors up ahead, frantically turned the doorknob, and slipped inside the room.

The door slammed shut. I stood still for a moment, catching my breath, and wondering what to do next.

"Hey, dude, what's up?" I turned and there was Izzy behind me, towering above me, a tube of rolled-up papers in his fist.

I hesitated and he narrowed his eyes at me. "You didn't follow that Ragg kid, did you? You did! Oh man, what are you thinking?"

"Listen, it's the weirdest thing," I said. I told him how Mason had looked so terrified of me, and how he had run like crazy when he saw I was behind him. We were both completely flummoxed.

"Maybe he's a werewolf, dude," Izzy said.

"Yeah, right," I said, but made a mental note to check if tonight was a full moon.

"And why would he leave you a note telling you to follow him if he was terrified when you actually did?" Izzy asked.

That was a good question.

"Maybe the note wasn't meant for me," I suggested. "Or maybe it was, but Mason wasn't the one who wrote it. Maybe I was supposed to follow someone else."

Behind us came the sound of a person clearing her throat. Izzy and I both jumped (the werewolf thing was still in our minds) and turned to see a teacher standing there with her hands on her hips.

"Let's go back to our classrooms, shall we?" she said.

"We shall," I said, because as you know, I always say stupid things when I'm nervous. The teacher narrowed her eyes at me and we hurried off.

Izzy walked me up to the second floor. He was hanging murals for the parent show, he told me, and he had to hang some up there anyway. He'd been hanging them all week as a matter of fact, which was great because he got out of class for half an hour or so. They chose him because he was so tall he could hang them without lugging around a chair.

Being a giant has its occasional advantages.

"Hey, man," Izzy said before we parted, "how about you just let Mason take those Oreos? What's the diff, you know?"

This echoed what Jeremy had said that morning. Everyone seemed to be turning on me at once.

"The *diff* is THEY'RE MY OREO COOKIES!" I cried.

Izzy held up his hands. "All right, all right, relax. See you at lunch."

He took off down the hall and I started walking back to my class. I passed right by the lunch closet, then I stopped. Backtracked.

I knew it was silly. I'd been right behind Mason so I knew that he didn't have time to rifle through my lunch, but I wanted to check anyway. I unrolled the tote bag and opened it up.

That's right. You guessed it.

My frickin' Oreo cookies were gone.

So it wasn't Mason after all.

12

It's funny the way things work. Just when I was thinking I might come close to a solution to my Mason Ragg problem, I found that I was even more confused than ever.

And just when I was feeling that I'd never be able to get Nemesis to work, a solution appeared out of the blue.

After school, I stopped by Nima's apartment. I hadn't seen him for a while, and quite frankly, I needed a break from Nemesis. I was afraid I was in for another long evening of Freakout shows with no sign of an old signal. Also, I was feeling pretty gloomy about the whole Jeremy thing and panicky about the whole Wooly thing, and I needed to take my mind off of both of them.

Nima was in the middle of watching one of his Indian movies, so he just opened the door, said a quick *tashi-deley*, and rushed back to the couch, where I sat down next to him. He's got about fifty of these Indian movies piled up in his closet. They're really goofy and they're all the same: there's a beautiful woman who's in love with a handsome man, and there's a bad guy who messes things up. Everyone sings and dances a few times, and it all works out great in the end. Nima loves these movies, which means I often have to sit through them. It's fairly excruciating for me. This time, I spent most of the movie counting how many times the bad guy stroked his moustache in this supposedly sinister way. Twenty-eight.

The actors suddenly exploded in a musical number, and everyone was dancing and spinning. It reminded me a little of that woman in front of the museum. Nima sang along in a loud, out-of-tune voice and started popping his head around like a chicken.

There was a close-up of the Indian actress singing something to her best girlfriend, her eyes looking all woozy, so I knew it must be something about the handsome guy. I snorted in disgust. Nima looked at me. I think he took it personally, he loves these movies so much. I didn't mean to hurt his feelings, so I tried to make an excuse for my snort.

"Pema is better-looking than that actress," I said.

"Pema is more beautiful than a jewel."

"Why doesn't she come here already?" I asked. I'd wanted to ask this for some time. I wasn't sure if it was some mysterious Tibetan custom, where you separate a newly wed husband and wife for a while.

"She wishes to. I wish her to. But her mother is sick, and there is no one to care for her but Pema. If I make more money, I can bring them both and pay for medicine for her mother. Maybe by next year."

"Next year!" I said.

"If business improve much."

Personally, I love momos. I think everyone should love momos. But lots of people have never heard of them, while everyone has heard of hot dogs or soft pretzels with mustard, both of which are sold at carts a few feet away from Nima's momo cart. It didn't seem likely that the momo business was going to suddenly skyrocket, but of course I didn't say that.

We watched to the end of the movie, although I really don't know why we bothered. They always end the same way. Just when you think all hope is lost, everything turns out great. The beautiful woman and the handsome guy get married while the bad guy gets punished.

"Let me ask you something, Nima," I said as the credits rolled. Nima was watching the credits with as much interest as he watched the movie. I'm telling you, he's a maniac when it comes to this stuff.

"Hmm?" he said, not taking his eyes off the screen.

"Do things ever turn out differently in these movies? Like the handsome guy gets killed, the beautiful woman gets depressed and gains two hundred pounds, and the bad guy never gets caught and lives happily ever after?"

"No, no, I don't think so," he said.

"Well, they should!" I said. "It's like false advertising or something. Real life is full of unhappy endings."

Nima nodded. "There is the saying, of course, life is not fair."

"It's not just a saying," I insisted glumly. "It's true."

"But in Buddhist belief, the bad guy always be punished. If not in this life, then in the next life."

"That's not soon enough," I grumbled.

Nima looked at me thoughtfully. Then he took a pack of cigarettes out of his shirt pocket, shook one out, and went to the window. He opened the window wide and sat on the sill while he smoked, careful to blow the smoke out into the cool early evening air. We were quiet for a while. I was deciding if I should tell him the truth about me, and I suspect he was simply waiting for me to decide.

"My parents owned a deli on Broadway and Eighty-fifth Street. It's a shoe store now," I said.

Nima turned away from the view outside the window and looked at me, his cigarette hand poised outside the window.

"They had really good knishes," I said. "You know what knishes are?"

"Like potato dumpling?" Nima said.

"Yeah, something like that. Anyway, it was just them, running the whole thing, and a guy who helped out on the weekends. They worked a lot. They didn't want to hand us over to a babysitter every night, so they fixed up a room for us in the deli's basement. Nothing fancy. Just an old sofa and a table for us to do our homework at, a TV, and two little cots. We liked it. It was sort of a clubhouse." It was so strange to be talking about this. My old life seemed to bloom before my eyes as I spoke. I could see that basement room so clearly—the cinder block walls, with each cinder block painted some crazy bright kid color. The shelf full of board games. The old yellow tent that we set up in the corner.

"Most nights Mom would take us home around eight and Dad would close up, but once a month Mom would stay late so she could take everything out of the coolers and wipe down the shelves. That night she was cleaning, so we were there late. Jeremy was sleeping already, but I was just lying down on my cot, thinking. Suddenly I heard yelling upstairs. I sat up in bed and listened. Sometimes homeless people would wander in the store, and some of them were sort of nutty, but my dad was really good at calming people down, giving them a little something to eat and sending them away. But this sounded different. The yelling came in short spurts. And it didn't stop. I looked over at Jeremy. She had the covers pulled up over her head and she was sound asleep. If she'd been awake, she would have run upstairs, I know she would have, but I didn't know what to do. The yelling grew louder and then I heard my mother yell back and then I heard a gunshot. Still, I just sat there. I was too scared to go up, too scared to move. Jeremy didn't wake up and I just sat there, I sat there like a rock, like a boulder. I sat there and let it all happen. Then there was another gunshot, and this time Jeremy woke up. She sat up in bed, her eyes all wide, and she said, 'What was that?'

"I didn't want to tell her. If I told her, she'd run upstairs and I would run after her and then we'd both be killed. So I told her that I thought it was the furnace."

I glanced over at Nima to check his expression. He didn't look appalled. I went on.

"After that there were some thumping noises, like stuff was being thrown around. Jeremy got out of bed and started for the stairs. I ran after her, and grabbed her to stop her, but she squirmed out of my grasp and ran up the stairs. Her hair was long, just like it is now, because our mother told her to wear it like a badge of honor, so I grabbed it and held her back just before she opened the door. Then I ran by her and at the top of the stairs I blocked the door that led out into the deli. She was pounding on me, trying to get around me, but I wouldn't move. I just stood there and wouldn't let her by. I was afraid the man was still out there. Jeremy started to scream, but I quickly clamped my hand over her mouth and held it there while I waited. I don't know how long I waited. It felt like hours. It was probably minutes. Then everything went quiet. Completely quiet. I opened the door. You could hear the hum of the cooler, it was so silent. My parents were lying on the floor behind the counter. It was—" I felt my lips crumpling, so I put my hand in front of my mouth to hide it.

"No need to say," Nima said, slipping off the sill and shutting the window. He tossed the cigarette butt in a glass and sat down beside me on the couch.

I felt a terrible ache in my throat, but I wanted to finish. "I called 911. It was Zelda who answered. Her voice . . . well, it's like when you are a little kid and have a nightmare and you're trembling and your mother holds you close and tells you that everything will be fine, and you just sink into her voice, just sink. She stayed on the phone with me until the police came. She kept telling me that I had done the right thing. She meant about holding Jeremy back from bursting into the deli. I didn't tell her everything. I didn't tell her that I had heard the screaming and the two gunshots and didn't do anything. I never told Jeremy either. I think she would have hated me.

"Later Zelda tracked us down. She told me that she couldn't stop thinking about us. She hears all kinds of awful stuff every day, but she said that my voice haunted her. I never told her, but her voice haunted me too. Whenever I started to think about that night, just as the memory started to get unbearable, her voice would break in and wrap itself around me and protect me.

"We had nowhere to go to, no relatives, just a grandmother who was in a nursing home. Zelda stepped up and said she'd take us in. Because of her job, she knew people who were able to speed things up and keep me and Jeremy out of foster care. She adopted us legally last January. She didn't *make* us call her 'Mom' or anything but she said we could if we wanted to. Jeremy never wanted to. She doesn't have the same feelings toward Zelda as I do. She wasn't the one who spoke to her that night. But I told Jeremy that we should at least try to call her Mom. After everything she's done for us."

"They did not catch the man who did this?" Nima asked quietly.

"There were no witnesses. It was late at night, and cold, so there weren't that many people on the street. The magazine store next door was closed, and so was the clothing store on the other side of the deli. The people in the building upstairs had heard gunshots, but no one had seen anything. We had a surveillance camera, a good one, wireless. But my parents weren't really good about checking it every so often to make sure everything was working. One of them must have taken out the tape at one point and forgotten to replace it. The camera had caught the event, but there was no tape in the machine to record it. So that was that. It looked like the man would never be caught. Then I saw the show about the ghosts in The Black Baron Pub, and I remembered that I still had the deli's surveillance camera system. I figured if I could build a radio telescope and hook it up to the surveillance camera's receiver, I had a chance at recapturing that old signal. Of seeing his face. So I built my radio telescope. And right now I've got a whole boxful of old television guides to help me figure out the dates of any old signals that Nemesis might pick up."

"And?" he said. "How she is working?"

I shook my head.

"She not work?" he asked.

"The signals aren't coming in strongly enough. I think I need a low-noise amplifier but I'm not sure. Maybe a bigger satellite dish. Or maybe it's all just impossible."

"Mmm." He thought for a moment. "Do you mind if I say prayer?"

"I don't know." I shrugged. "I'm not religious, but I guess it would be okay."

Nima sat down in front of his shrine and said many things in Tibetan. It sounded like he was chanting. It was a strange sound. Sort of soothing. The Dalai Lama kept staring at me from his portrait, smiling like he was remembering something funny that happened a long time ago.

"What did you say?" I asked.

"I pray for your honored parents. Also, I pray for the man who killed your parents."

I wasn't sure I liked the last part of his prayer, but the rest was nice. I thanked him. He waved away the thanks.

Later, when Jeremy, Mom, and I were sitting down to dinner, there was a knock on our door. Mom got up to answer it. When I heard Nima's voice, I rushed to the door in time to see Mom do a little half bow and say, "Please come in." I think she had this idea that he was a monk or something because I told her about the shrine in his house.

"This come from my cousin's house," Nima said as he placed a piece of electronic equipment in my hands. "He bought a new one, so this one not necessary." It was a low-noise amplifier. A good one. And it looked new.

"Nima, you bought this! No, I can't take it." I held it back out to him. I knew how much those things cost, and it was more than a momo maker should spend. Especially one who is saving his money to bring his wife and sick mother-in-law to America.

"No, no," He stepped back, away from it. "My cousin. He not need it."

"I don't believe you for a minute," I said.

"Ms. Birnbaum," Nima said to Mom, "please tell Owen that Buddhists do not tell lies."

"Owen, you're offending him," Mom hissed at me, horrified. That made Nima smile, the good-natured pirate smile.

I knew he was lying.

But I needed the amplifier.

"I'll find a way to pay you back," I said to Nima.

Mom asked him to come in and join us for stuffed squash surprise and he agreed happily, which was pretty brave in my opinion.

FYI, it is said that the Buddha died of food poisoning after eating at someone's house.

Nima actually cleaned his plate and asked Mom what the brown, chewy things were, and she told him it was tempeh.

"Which is really just a fancy term for blechh!" Jeremy said. Then added, "Sorry, Mom."

Did you catch that? She said *Mom*.

Mom smiled as she said, "No problem, Jeremy."

It was one of those gooey moments that we were all embarrassed by, so Jeremy put a piece of tempeh on Honey's nose and we watched her flip it in the air and catch it in her mouth. It's the only trick that she can do.

After dinner I hooked up the low-noise amplifier and

turned on the Freakout Channel. Then I did one more thing. I opened my desk drawer and pulled out the little slip of paper with SLOB written on it. Carefully I placed it under the new amplifier. It was an offering, like Nima's offerings at his shrine. A sort of prayer.

A two-hour *Love Boat* special was being aired on the Freakout Channel. This was going to be a long night. I watched for a solid hour until I finally couldn't take it any longer and I took out my English homework. Every so often I glanced up listlessly to catch a glimpse of what was happening on the show before sticking my nose back in my homework.

Then something happened.

You know when you are walking along, minding your own business, and you suddenly trip and fall on your face? For that half second when your feet are no longer touching the ground, everything is in slow motion and you think, Wow, this is bizarre.

That's what happened when the TV made a little *pift* sound and suddenly *Charlie's Angels* was on. The picture was pretty fuzzy, just like the ghost images at The Black Baron Pub. I stared at the TV for a second or two and actually said out loud, "What? What's hap—what?"

My eyes grew wider as I watched a blond Charlie's Angel jumping around, dressed as a cheerleader.

"Okay, Okay, this is it, Owen," I said, still talking out loud. I needed to hear my own voice to convince myself this was real.

My heart was thumping harder than any thump that Andre had ever given me. This was it. I had done it! Me, twelve-year-old Owen Birnbaum, had done it with junkyard scraps and brainpower. And Nima's amplifier, of course. The feeling of success was so overwhelming that for a while I nearly forgot what all this hard work had been for.

Okay, I said to myself. Calm down. You may have managed to get an old signal but now you have to figure out when that signal was first sent out. I'd have to check the old *Retro TV Magazines* for the dates on which that episode was shown. Chances were they'd shown that episode more than once in the past two years. After that, I'd still have to capture some more old signals and recheck the magazines to pinpoint the dates of these old signals. If they were from before October 25, 2006, the day my parents were killed, I still had time to possibly capture the surveillance recording from that night. I could hook up the deli's surveillance camera receiver to Nemesis and start looking. But if the signals were from after that date, it was all for nothing. Well, Nemesis would be a success, but any hope of identifying the person who had shot my parents would be lost forever. I ran to Jeremy's room and pounded on the door.

"What?" she yelled on the other side of the door.

"Come in my room and look," I called, and rushed back to my bedroom.

In a minute she came in my room and stared at the TV.

"*Charlie's Angels*. Stupid show," she said.

"But I was watching *The Love Boat*."

She stared at me for a second, then her eyes went wide. "You mean it worked?"

I nodded.

"You did it?" Her voice was getting shrill.

I nodded again.

"I can't believe it. Owen! You are a total genius!"

Almost.

Still, I loved the way she said that.

We watched the show for ten more minutes, though Jeremy kept making gagging noises whenever the cheerleaders appeared. Suddenly the TV went *pift* and *The Love Boat* came back on.

Crap.

I ran up to Nemesis and checked the equipment. Everything looked fine. I had simply lost the signal.

"Do you think it will come back again tonight?" Jeremy asked.

"I don't know."

"Well, there's no school tomorrow . . . Teachers' Conference Day. You can watch the Freakout Channel all day long to see if you can catch the signal again."

I shook my head. "It doesn't work like that. I won't be able to catch the signal until around the same time tomorrow night. Come here, I'll show you."

Jeremy came to the window, and I pointed out into the black, star-freckled sky.

"See that star up there?" I said. "Between the water tower and the Fuji Towers?"

She nodded.

"Pretend that's the Nemesis star. It's not, but just imagine. That star will only be in that particular spot for a certain amount of time this evening. Soon it will pass out of sight behind that water tower. Tomorrow night, at around this time, it will be there again for a while, although over weeks it will drift a little. When *Charlie's Angels* came on, the Nemesis star was at just the right spot for me to catch signals off of it. I'll have to wait until around the same time tomorrow night to get the signals again. *If* I can get them again. Understand?"

"Got it." She nodded once, although she looked so confused that I doubted she really did.

"But," she said after a moment of thought, "how will you know when that old *Charlie's Angels* episode aired two years ago?"

"I'll have to go through all the *Retro TV Magazine*s and write down the day and time the episode was on. If I'm lucky, it will only have been on once in the past two years. If not, I'll have to make a list of all the dates and times it was on. Then I'll try to pick up an old signal tomorrow. Let's say I manage to pick up an old episode of *I Love Lucy*. I'll have to go through all the guides again, find that particular episode of *I Love Lucy*, and pinpoint the day on which it was aired a day after the cheerleader episode of *Charlie's Angels*. Then I've got my date."

"Oh," she said. "All right." It was hard to know if she understood what I was talking about. She left the room then, and I sat back down and watched the Freakout Channel for a little longer, just in case. No luck.

All right, all right, I told myself. No big deal. I had my episode. The angels were posing as cheerleaders to catch a bunch of kidnappers. Now I could look it up in *Retro TV Magazine* and figure out what date it was aired on.

I went to the box full of magazines and knelt beside it. I even remembered to put on the white gloves. That was when I realized exactly what a task lay before me. I had to leaf through 104 issues and hunt down every *Charlie's Angels* episode. I made it through forty-eight issues before I fell asleep sitting up in bed, my back propped against the wall and the white gloves still on my hands.

13

In the morning I woke up late and went out to the kitchen to eat a bowl of Cocoa Puffs cereal with milk. Actually, it was the fake Cocoa Puffs, with the organic this and that, and it tastes almost nothing like the real Cocoa Puffs, but that morning I hardly noticed. I was too anxious to get back to the *Retro TV Magazine* issues. I even took a couple of the issues into the kitchen with me, and after I finished my cereal, I put the white gloves on and began to search through them again.

Jeremy came into the kitchen wearing her jacket and a black ski cap pulled down around her ears. Her ice skates were slung over one shoulder. She stood in the doorway and watched me for a minute.

"I'm going skating with Arthur," she said.

I waited for her to ask me if I wanted to come. She didn't. Again, I felt her watching me.

"What?" I said.

"I was just thinking," she said. "Even if you see the

person who did it, even if the police can find him and catch him and stick him in jail, it won't change things. Not really."

"How can you say that? Of course it will change things!" I said.

"It won't change things for us, I mean," she said. "Or for Mom and Dad. It won't make them less dead."

"It will change things for the person who killed them, won't it?" I said. My voice sounded all strangled, I was so angry. "Living in a prison cell for the rest of your life is a pretty big change, in my opinion. Jeez, Jeremy, I would have thought you of all people would see why this is so important!"

"It's just—"

"It's just that now you have a bunch of friends and you and Zelda are getting along, so everything is fine, right? Well things are not fine for me, in case you haven't noticed. Things are pretty lousy, if you want to know the truth. I'm the butt of everyone's jokes, someone is helping themself to my lunch, and Mr. Wooly is going to humiliate me in front of the entire class. Yet again."

I knew what she was going to say—that even if the murderer was caught, people were not going to stop making fun of me. That I would still be 57 percent fatter than the average American twelve-year-old.

That's not what she said.

She didn't say anything. She just hiked up her skates higher on her shoulder and left the apartment.

The whole thing bothered me so much that I ripped off the white gloves, poured another bowlful of fake Cocoa Puffs, and scarfed it down. After that, I fished around the fridge until I found half a turkey sub that Mom had brought home from work and began to devour that too. My stomach was suddenly gripped with the familiar aching emptiness that came on right before a major food binge. The first time I had felt it was a few months after my parents were killed. Back then I ate a half pint of rocky road ice cream, and that made it better. After a while it would take a whole pint to fill the emptiness. Then a pint and a Snickers bar, and on and on. The way I was feeling now, I could make a clean sweep of a five-gallon drum of ice cream and still have room for a family-sized bag of pretzels. I was still chewing on the final bite of the sub and was just getting up to rummage through the kitchen cabinets for more food when I caught sight of the white gloves lying on the stack of *Retro TV Magazine*s. One glove lay on top of the other, just like two hands that were patiently waiting on their owner's lap. Very narrow, delicate hands. It made me think of my mother's own hands—long and slender and pale— and I shivered. At that moment it felt like she was sitting right there, across from me, waiting to see what I would do next.

I stood there for a second, staring at the gloves and feeling the awful ache in my belly. Then I sat back down again. I slipped on the gloves, picked up an issue of *Retro TV Magazine*, and resumed my search for the cheerleader episode of *Charlie's Angels*. The painful feeling in my gut didn't leave. If anything, it grew worse, but I just kept my butt planted in that chair and the gloves on my hand. As long as the gloves were on my hands, I reasoned, I could not eat.

I finished my search at a little past eleven. To my dismay, I found that the episode, called *Pom Pom Angels,* was on a total of twenty-three times in the past two years! I hadn't counted on that. No doubt that particular episode was so popular because of the cheerleaders.

Well, I would just have to catch some more old signals, and with any luck they would be from really unpopular shows that were aired only once in the past two years.

I watched the Freakout Channel until three thirty. I was watching out of habit, really, since I now knew that the signal from Nemesis wouldn't come in until the evening. At three thirty I took Honey out for a walk and came back and watched more TV until Mom said dinner was ready. My eyes were burning from watching all that TV, and I felt slightly nauseated. Apparently Jeremy was not feeling so good herself. She had come back from ice skating around four and hadn't been out of her room since.

"Go tell Jeremy that dinner is ready," Mom said as she gave the salmon burgers a final flip.

I knocked on her door. "Jeremy. Dinner."

"I'm not hungry," she called back.

"You all right?"

"Yes," she said. Then added, "I'm sleeping."

"She's sleeping," I told Mom.

"Really? Is she sick?" I could practically hear Mom sorting through her brain's stockpile of teas with healing properties.

"I think she's just tired," I said. Actually, I guessed she was mad about this morning, and that made *me* mad. She was the one who was being difficult. I suspected she was jealous, although I never would have thought her to be that type. People change, though. She should have just been thankful, she should be thinking of something more than herself. She should be thinking about our mom and dad and doing what was right.

After dinner I went back into my room and into the world of Freakout. By now, I probably knew just as much about these shows as Arthur. Speaking of which, when I turned on the TV, an episode of *Happy Days* was playing. After watching a few episodes, I was beginning to get the appeal of The Fonz. He was tough on the outside and nice on the inside. People love that. Somehow it's even better than being nice all over.

Then came *B.J. and the Bear,* which is about a truck driver and a chimpanzee. Yes, it is as stupid as it sounds. And wouldn't you know it, they had a marathon that night. Three *B.J. and the Bear* episodes in a row. I didn't know if I could stand it. I pulled the scavenged junk box out of the closet and started messing around with some of the items, just for something to do. I picked up an old bike chain and turned it over in my hands. I'd always wanted to do something with it, but I never could think what.

Suddenly there was *pift*.

My heart jumped and my head shot up. On TV a fuzzy Jan Brady was sneezing like mad. I watched long enough to get the gist of the plotline (six minutes). Jan was allergic to the family dog, Tiger, and they were going to have to get rid of him.

Okay. We were back in business. Now I had to slip on the white gloves again and start studying two years' worth of *Retro TV Magazine* for every instance of *The Brady Bunch* on the Freakout Channel. Plus, there was a very good chance that this episode had been repeated several times. If only I had been able to catch two old episodes in a row, I would have a better chance at figuring out when these shows were first broadcast. But since there was no guarantee that I'd hold onto the signal for that long, I went to Arthur's carton and started my long night's work.

Then I got lucky.

There was a commercial break on TV, and a fuzzy lime green screen came on with the words *Freakout Pop Quiz* in hot pink bubble letters. Then a voice read out the pop quiz question while it was spelled out on-screen: "What famous *Laverne and Shirley* star was born on this day, sixty-three years ago?"

I waited through a bunch of commercials, terrified every second that I'd lose the signal before the answer came on. I didn't. "The answer to today's Freakout Pop Quiz is . . . Penny Marshall, who played Laverne on *Laverne and Shirley.*"

I was so happy I could have done that embarrassing little dance.

Now all I had to do was to check the Internet for Penny Marshall's birthday. Once I found that out, I just had to do a simple calculation to figure out the day, month, and year of this broadcast. Presto!

Well, not quite *presto* since we didn't have the Internet at home. I'd have to wait till I got to school to check it.

Pift.

Jan Brady was gone, and in her place was a chimpanzee doing a handstand on a pool table.

I'd lost the signal.

Jeremy left for school without me the next morning. She must have snuck out while I was in the shower, because her door was closed when I walked into the bathroom and when I came out, the door was open and she was gone. She'd never left without me before, and I won't lie, it hurt my feelings. At first. Then it just started making me angrier with her, and by the time I got to school, I decided that I wouldn't wait for her after school. I just hoped that she would notice.

I arrived at school early to sign up for the computer workstation. There's only one computer in our classroom, and it's hooked up to the Internet, so it's always the most popular workstation. I was the first one on the list today. I was shaking with nervousness. Everything rested on this one piece of information.

Mason Ragg slunk in, late as usual. He looked the same as always—from the top of his wild uncombed head to the tips of his busted-up sneakers, every inch of him seemed to say, "Oh yeah? Go ahead, I dare you." It was almost unbelievable to me that only the day before yesterday, I had seen him fleeing from me with terror in his face.

He caught me staring at him, but this time his eyes swerved away quickly.

For no reason at all, I felt like a bully.

Well, maybe there was a tiny reason.

I started thinking about this whole karma thing. It occurred to me that I might have collected some pretty rotten karma lately. After all, I had attempted to clap Mason's wrist in a spiked handcuff and possibly poison him with facial hair bleach, and the whole time he was innocent. I assumed that these were fairly serious crimes, karma-wise.

I looked at the computer screen as it was slowly booting up. If I ever needed some good karma, it was now.

I stood up and walked over to Mason, who was sitting in the art station, drawing on a piece of paper. His back was to me, so I was able to get a good look at his drawing. It was a wolf howling.

"Wow, that's good," I said. It really was. The wolf's fur was drawn with these careful, fine little strokes. It was hard to believe Mason could do something that delicate.

Mason's head swiveled around. Thankfully I had a view of the unscarred side of his face this time. It was like the half man/half woman that you'd see in old-time circus pictures. He gave a totally different impression if you saw him from the left side or from the right. From this view, Mason Ragg just looked like an unkempt kid. Nothing sinister in the slightest.

"I don't have your (really bad curse word) cookies, if that's what you want," he said.

"I know you don't," I told him.

"Then what do you want?" He didn't look mad. He looked nervous. Of *me!* Owen Birnbaum. Professional Boulder.

"I want Penny Marshall's birthday to be before October 25."

No, I didn't say that.

"I want to tell you something," I said. An opportunity for improving my karma had just popped into my head. "First of all, could you still be exempt from going to gym class?"

"I guess," he said cagily. "If I wanted to be."

"Then ask for an exemption today," I said.

"Why?"

"Because Wooly has it out for us," I said. From the corner of my eye, I could see the computer screen light up and the little *ta-dring* sound. "He thinks that we somehow knew there was going to be a fire drill on Friday and we deliberately put ourselves last so we could get out of the triathlon. He's going to make us do something totally humiliating today, you can count on it."

This didn't seem to impress Mason the way I had hoped.

He turned back to his drawing and started working on it again.

"I *did* know," he said.

"Know what?"

"I knew about the fire drill."

"But how?" I asked.

"I hear things," he answered mysteriously.

"So you put us last deliberately?" I asked.

Mason nodded. His pen was adding tiny slashes of fur to the wolf's cheek.

Two things occurred to me:

1. I had really misjudged Mason. He was actually a pretty nice guy.
2. I had a hell of a lot of work to do in the bad karma department.

"Everyone wanted to see you make a clown of yourself," Mason explained. He drew a full moon in the left corner of the page. "I hate clowns," he said.

Oh.

Well, maybe I had slightly less work to do in the karma department.

"Anyway," I said, edging toward the computer station, "just remember about the exemption."

He nodded without looking up.

I walked away hoping it was enough to erase all the bad stuff I had done. It *felt* like it was enough. In fact, I thought it was downright heroic considering that when Wooly saw that Mason wasn't in gym class, he'd pour out all his wrath on me. And believe me, I'm no hero.

I sat down in front of the computer and signed on to the Internet. I typed in *penny marshall birthday* in the search engine. Before I hit Enter, I took a deep breath, closed my eyes and thought, Pleasepleaseplease.

Then I hit Enter.

There it was, right on top of the page. I didn't even have to click on a website. *Penny Marshall Date of Birth Oct. 15, 1943.*

I did the math. That *Brady Bunch* episode was aired on October 15, 2006. Ten days before my parents were killed. The timing was right. It was perfect, in fact, since it gave me ten days to hook Nemesis up to the deli's surveillance camera receiver and attempt to capture the signals from the night of October 25.

Amazing what some good karma could do.

Now I just had to get through gym class.

I stayed at the computer workstation for twenty minutes, looking up stuff about hieroglyphics for my paper, because Rachel was interested in them and I was hoping to impress her.

As 11:40 crept closer, I began to feel queasy—so queasy, in fact, that I considered telling Ms. Bussle that I was sick again and needed to go home. The idea began to appeal to me. No gym class. No public humiliation.

It would also give me an entire day at home to work on Nemesis. That was much more important than anything I was going to do in school today.

"I feel queasy," I said to Ms. Bussle very quietly. I didn't want Mason to hear. For now, he might actually think that I was brave enough to face Wooly on my own. Of course by tomorrow he'd know that I was in fact the biggest coward in the Northern Hemisphere, but I wasn't thinking about tomorrow. Or even about two hours from now. I was thinking about 11:40, which was in exactly fifteen minutes.

Ms. Bussle squinted at me suspiciously. She was going to give me a hard time, I could tell. And it was going to be in a loud voice. I quickly clapped my hand over my mouth and made a small lurching movement with my neck, as though I was about to puke right then and there.

That wasn't one of my finer moments.

It worked, though. Ms. Bussle handed me the hall pass right away, and I hurried out before she could change her mind. I went directly through the hall and to the stairwell, but then I stopped. I was beginning to have second thoughts about this being the best-possible course of action.

I heard heels clicking down the hall, so I slipped inside the boys' bathroom. Thankfully it just smelled like disinfectant and nothing worse. I sat on the shallow tiled windowsill, leaned my head against the thick frosted glass, and sorted through my thoughts.

Here's what they were:

If both Mason and I missed gym class today, Wooly was going to be a raving monster on Friday.

Friday was only two days away.

On the other hand, anything could happen to Wooly in two days. A freak accident, debilitating illness, short-term memory loss, a change of heart.

None of which were statistically likely.

On the other hand—

I checked my watch. It was 11: 35.

Decide, decide. I groaned. The water pipes above me groaned back. They really did. I glanced up at them, and that's when I saw the grayish white thing hanging from a piece of hooked wire on one of the ceiling pipes. At first I thought it was someone's old underwear. Then I looked more carefully. I sucked in my breath. It was my lunch sack. My recycled sock lunch sack. Just hanging on that wire by its small cloth loop, like a dead cat. It felt so personal, like someone had hung *me* up there for everyone to see, drooping and helpless. Look, it seemed to say! This is what you can do to Owen Birnbaum. He'll let you do it. He won't make a stink. He won't fight back.

Then I had a thought that was more horrible yet.

The wire was really high up. Definitely more than six feet off the ground. There were no chairs to stand on in the bathroom. It would be nearly impossible to throw the sack in the air and have the wire hook catch the tiny little loop on the outside of the sack by pure chance. Someone had hung the sack up there deliberately. Someone very tall.

Someone who had free access to all the hallways this past week while he was taping up murals for the parent show.

Someone who could have rifled through the lunch closet, no problem.

I suddenly remembered what Jeremy had said to me: *I've heard people laugh at you. They make you the butt of their jokes in front of everybody, even though they're friends.*

I had thought she meant that they were *her* friends. But maybe she meant that they were *mine*. My only friend, as a matter of fact, besides Nima.

Something came out of my mouth then that can only be described as a yowl. It rebounded off the bathroom's tiled walls and sounded so much like an animal in some sort of anguish that I listened to its echo in shock.

That was me, I thought in amazement.

"What was that?" A kid had poked his head into the bathroom and was staring at me. I knew him. He was in my gym class. He must be on his way there now.

A breeze came in from the hallway, and I saw my lunch sack flutter slightly like a flag.

Owen Birnbaum's flag. The Republic of the Big Fat Boulder. Long may it wave.

I jumped off the windowsill, pushed past the kid in the doorway, and headed to gym class.

14

I felt pretty brave until I started pulling on my gym shorts. Then I started trembling. It was the sort of trembling that I'm not sure you can see from the outside. It was deep, deep inside. The kind you can hear in your breath.

As usual I was the last one in to the gym. All the kids were in a state of confusion. No one was standing on their spots for the simple reason that 80 percent of the gym was covered with gym equipment. Wooly must have pulled out everything in the equipment storage room—trampoline, mats, hurdles, tires set up on their sides, tires set up as a tunnel.

Faced with this buffet of torture, you can see why it took me a few moments to realize that everyone was watching me. Word must have gotten around about Wooly's plans.

Thanks, Andre.

"Oh, man, Flapjack." Andre sidled up to me and thumped me in the ribs. "Why didn't you get the damn exemption? Are you a glutton for punishment or something?"

I waited for someone to riff on the word *glutton*, but no one did. That's how serious the situation was.

I saw Wooly stop momentarily in his fussing with the equipment and scan the group. His eyes landed on mine. His chin lifted slightly and his ape chest puffed out. He had sighed. Yes, he was a happy man. Next, his glance flitted over to my left and seemed to be searching for something. He must have found it because his face grew stony. I looked to see what he was staring at, as did everyone in the class, and found the wiry figure slouching at the far end of the group.

Mason Ragg.

When you are looking down the barrel of your own imminent pain and suffering, you can't help but feel relieved that you have someone to share it with. I know that's not very Buddhist of me, but it's the truth.

I tried to save him. Don't forget that.

I did it for karma points, however.

Note to self: Ask Nima if good karma can be revoked, like a driver's license.

I made my way through the group until I was standing next to Mason. He was the only other person in this crowd who might be experiencing a similar sense of doom, and I felt a natural inclination to be near him. Also, I hadn't forgotten the switchblade in his sock. Not that I thought he would use it or anything. It just seemed like a situation where you would want to be near a person who carried a switchblade in his sock.

I wound up on the evil genius side of his face, but for some reason it didn't give me the heebie-jeebies. In fact, when I looked at him, I found that I was mentally skipping over the scar somehow.

"Is this all for us?" he asked in a quiet voice.

"I'm pretty sure," I answered. "How come you didn't get an exemption?"

Mason shrugged. "I wasn't in the mood. What do you guess all the mats are for?"

"Somersaults."

"Can you do one?" he asked.

I remembered that Mason hadn't been there to witness the dog harness.

I nodded. I did think I could, actually. As I said before, it's all physics.

"Good." Mason nodded slowly. "How about jumping hurdles?"

"Not my specialty," I said.

"That's what I figured. Trampoline?"

"Don't know."

"I bet not good," Mason said.

"Probably not," I agreed. I wasn't insulted by all this, though. Mason didn't seem to be making fun of me. The whole time he'd been eyeing the equipment thoughtfully, as though he were working something out.

"Those tires, the ones standing upright, are the things that worry me the most though," he said.

"Really?" I said, surprised. There were four of the tires

standing up and permanently fixed to a plank of wood. "Don't worry. You'll crawl through those, no problem."

Mason looked at me. I was getting so used to the evil genius side of his face that now I could even figure out its expressions. At the moment it looked like it couldn't believe how thickheaded I was.

"I'm not nervous for me, I'm nervous for *you,*" he said. "You'll *never* squeeze through those tires. In fact, I could see you getting wedged in there and not being able to get out. I'm sure Wooly thought of that too."

I took a better look at the tires. I hadn't thought about them too much because they looked so harmless compared to the rest of the stuff. Mason was right. The centers were small, so small that some of the average-sized kids in the class would have a hard time fitting through. As you are well aware, I am not average size.

"See," Mason continued, "he put them at the end of the obstacle course. It's like the grand finale, you getting stuck in there."

"Holy crap, you're right." That was just what Wooly would do! "How did you know that?"

"I've dealt with people like him before. Worse than him." Mason said grimly. "So here's how you handle this. You do the somersaults. You do the hurdles. You'll knock them over but lots of people do, just try not to fall on your face. The trampoline is going to be tricky. No matter what you do, people are going to laugh at you while you're on it. Fat kid bouncing around, you know. Make one really good bounce, and when you hit the trampoline, start screaming that you've hurt your ankle. It happens all the time. Even Wooly won't try and make you keep going if you're injured, and you'll have gotten through at least half of the obstacle course without making a total fool of yourself. It will be bad, I'm not going to lie, but at least you'll avoid getting stuck in those tires."

I stared at him in astonishment. His eyes shot away from mine.

"Let's just say I've spent most of my life avoiding humiliation," he muttered by way of an explanation.

I couldn't help it. Thoughts of werewolves went through my mind.

I wasn't astonished at his plan, though, as good as it was. I was astonished that he had thought this all out for *me!* He had shown up for gym even though he didn't have to, and faced with Wooly's diabolical obstacle course, he was more concerned about me than he was about himself.

Personally, I was beginning to think that Mason Ragg might be a little like The Fonz. Tough on the outside but heart of gold on the inside. Practically the very next second, the gym door opened and in marched Arthur. No kidding. It was like she had ultrasonic hearing for anything related to The Fonz and would appear on the spot if someone even thought about him. Stranger still, she was dressed in a boy's gym uniform—white T-shirt, blue shorts. Right behind her was Jennifer Crawford, a.k.a. Benjamin, then came Emmie Wiltshire, a.k.a. Robert, then Chantal Samms, a.k.a. George, then three more members of GWAB whose names I didn't know. They were all dressed in boys' uniforms. I don't know where they got them from, but except for Arthur, they didn't fit the GWAB members very well. Then came Sybil Tushman with her camcorder. Last of all came Jeremy. I knew she would be there, of course. It came to me in a flash that this was The Blue and White Rebellion they had been plotting (blue and white being the colors of the gym uniforms), and now I realized with horror that she was going to watch Wooly wipe the floor with me. And so were her friends. If she was ashamed of me before this, she was going to want to disown me as a brother after this debacle.

Jeremy's gym uniform was so big that the shorts reached below her knees, and the T-shirt was almost as long as the shorts. But what shocked me, what made me literally suck back my breath in a gasp, was her hair. The long red mane that she had always refused to cut because our mother had loved it so much had been completely lopped off. Her hair was as short as a boy's. It struck me as the final betrayal. With a few bold snips of the scissors, she had cut us all out, along with her hair—Mom, Dad. Me.

Still, I didn't think she looked very happy as she followed the others to the back end of the gym where we all stood, gawping at them (for the moment, everyone had forgotten about me and Mason and every head was riveted to the GWAB parade). Her head was lowered and her eyebrows were pinched together. She looked mad. Fighting mad. By comparison, the other girls just looked like they were pretending to be angry, but mostly they looked self-conscious as they stood in a clump by the rest of us, tugging at their badly fitting uniforms.

Suddenly I had two thoughts:

1. Watch out, Arthur. Jeremy is going to become the president of GWAB in no time.
2. The Blue and White Rebellion might actually save the day. Wooly was going to have to deal with them, and that would eat up precious pain-and-suffering time that he'd allotted for me and Mason.

I considered donating a charitable contribution to the organization.

Like the rest of us, Mr. Wooly watched the members of GWAB in bewildered silence. Then he collected himself and boomed:

"Excuse me, ladies!"

Our class was so used to being called "ladies" that all our heads turned toward him. So he made a lassoing motion with his arm in the direction of the GWAB members and clarified things by saying, "You lot! The girls in boys' uniforms! Out!" His invisible lasso was now tossed toward the gym doors.

Arthur stepped forward. It wasn't a big step and it probably should have been. She started saying something. I

was pretty sure it was the speech that they had been working on. Unfortunately, no one could hear what she was
saying.

"I can't hear what you're saying," Mr. Wooly said.

Arthur started again, a little more loudly but not loud
enough.

"What? What are you mumbling about?" Mr. Wooly
said.

This was all working out so well, I could have hugged
Arthur, I really could have. Time was ticking away.

All of a sudden Jeremy stepped forward. It was a big
step. A decisive step. It was the step of a soon-to-be GWAB
president.

"We, the members of GWAB, demand to be recognized
by our true identities . . ."

It was the GWAB statement they had been working on.
Jeremy recited it very well in a loud clear voice that Mr.
Wooly could completely understand. The only problem
with the speech, from my perspective, was that it wouldn't
go on long enough. Still, I calculated that there would be
plenty more time wasted while Mr. Wooly tried to get them
to leave voluntarily (good luck with that), then called someone in to forcibly escort them out, then waited for said person to arrive, etc. It was all shaping up perfectly.

I glanced over at Mason to see if he was as happy about
this new development as I was. He didn't seem to be. He
wasn't even looking at Jeremy and Wooly. Instead he was

concentrating on something in the far corner of the gymnasium ceiling. I followed his glance, but I couldn't for the life of me figure out what was so interesting up there.

"... demand to be included in the boys' section of gym class and to—"

"You're Birnbaum's sister, aren't you?" Mr. Wooly interrupted her.

My happiness screeched to a grinding halt.

For the first time since she'd walked in, Jeremy looked unsure of herself. She was silent for a moment, and I could see her blinking a little too quickly. If she said "No" it would crush me. But I also felt nervous about her saying "Yes."

No good could come of this, I was sure.

Jeremy jerked her head quickly to one side, which was a gesture she often made to swish her long hair off her shoulder. Of course now there was nothing to swish.

"Owen's my brother," she said cautiously.

"Well, that's just marvelous!" Mr. Wooly slapped his hands together. "Perfect timing! All right, let's get on with business."

"But I didn't finish," Jeremy objected.

"Oh, I got the gist. You all want to be treated like boys, blabbedy blah. All right, today is your lucky day. You gals will be our honored guests. Where's the kid with the camera? You're recording all this for posterity, right?"

"For my video blog, *The Universe According to Sybil*," Sybil Tushman said.

"Even better! Well then come up front by me, that's right. You'll get a better view of the action from here." He ushered Sybil up front with the greatest respect, guiding her past all the obstacles on the floor.

"Today, ladies"—now he meant all of us—"we have a special treat. Because Mr. Birnbaum and Mr. Ragg were unable to complete the triathlon on Friday, I've organized a special event just for them. I hope the members of GLOB enjoy this demonstration, as well as"—he flourished a hand toward Sybil—"the fans of your video thing. Do you have a lot of fans, by the way?"

"A decent amount," Sybil said.

"Nice," Mr. Wooly said, smiling. By tonight, most of the school would be watching me tripping over hurdles and flopping around on a trampoline. Rachel Lowry included. Things couldn't have worked out better for Mr. Wooly if he had planned The Blue and White Rebellion himself. I wondered if my good karma points *had* been revoked and been transferred to Mr. Wooly. I couldn't imagine any other way that he might have gotten his hands on some good karma.

I looked over at Jeremy. She was staring back at me, her expression full of something big, but what? Fear, anger? I couldn't tell.

Well, Jeremy, I thought, now you are going to see it firsthand. This is what my life is like. This is who I am now. The big, fat kid. Fatty Fatty Ding Dong.

You're not Caitlin anymore, and I'm not Owen. Not *that* Owen anyway. Not the Owen that you used to know.

"Mr. Birnbaum! Mr. Ragg! Front and center!"

My guts twisted up and my mouth instantly went dry. I looked over at Mason. He looked terrified.

"I've got to get out of here!" he said to me in a panicked voice. "Now!" Then he started for the exit marked Boys', which led down to the boys' locker room.

"What are you talking about?" I grabbed him by his upper arm. Me. Owen Birnbaum grabbed Mason Ragg.

"Get off of me!" he shrieked, and pulled away, then hightailed it through the crowds, running toward the boys' exit door, nearly knocking down Justin Esposito in the process. I was so stunned that it took me a minute to realize what was happening. He had chickened out! All that talk was a load of nonsense. He was a coward, just like me! More of a coward, because I wasn't running away. I was scared, but I wouldn't run. At least I could be proud of that.

Nima says that when you start to feel like you are better than someone else, you should probably stick your head in a toilet because at that moment your thoughts are crap.

"Ragg! Get back here!" Mr. Wooly had caught sight of Mason trying to escape and started rushing toward him. The obstacle course slowed him down. He stumbled over the edge of a mat and crashed against a hurdle.

Suddenly, all the bravery that I had been able to muster evaporated. All the confidence that I had in Mason's plan crumbled.

You know what? I thought. I am just as much a coward as Mason.

That was when I started to run too.

"Birnbaum!" Wooly bellowed. "Don't you take another step!"

Mason reached the boys' exit door a minute before I did. He flung it open, and before it could completely swing back shut, we went through. There was a short set of stairs, then a hallway, and then another door that opened into the boys' lockers and showers. Mason was almost at the second door when I called out, "Why the hell did you show up, Mason, if you were only going to run away? Now you've just made everything worse! Wooly is madder than before—at both of us!"

Mason turned around. The expression on his face was the same one I had seen in the school hallway the other day. The look of wild panic.

"Don't let them see," he said before disappearing behind the locker room door.

"See what?" I cried.

Jeremy arrived then, her legs pounding down the stairs, and right after her Wooly stormed through. His face was a really alarming color, sort of a lavender, and a little speck of spit flew out of his mouth as he said, "Birnbaum, you are going to haul your carcass back in the gym right this second." He said it sort of quietly, which was scarier than his bellowing. "And where is Ragg?"

The door opened behind Wooly, and some of my classmates followed him cautiously, not wanting to get in the line of fire of Wooly's fury but also not wanting to miss out on any of the good stuff.

"Where's Ragg?!" Wooly repeated, this time in his usual bellow. "Is he in there?"

I didn't answer, so Wooly stepped forward to go through the locker room door. I stepped back and stood in front of it. From inside the locker room came the sound of a loud crash.

"What was that?" Jeremy whispered.

"I don't know," I whispered back. Before I could stop her, she opened the locker room door and slipped inside.

Instantly a cheer sounded from the top of the stairs. I looked up to see the members of GWAB hooting and punching their arms in the air. It took me a minute to realize why.

A GWAB member had infiltrated the boys' locker room. This moment would live forever in GWAB history, particularly since Sybil Tushman was filming it all at the top of the stairs.

"All right, Birnbaum, out of the way." Wooly made a movement toward the door, but I stayed put, spreading my arms wide so that I blocked the entire door.

Wooly let loose with a string of threats, ranging from calling in the principal to calling my mom to immediate suspension to making my life a living hell. I had no doubt he would do all those things. But in my mind, I could still see Mason's frightened, wild-looking eyes and hear his frantic words, "Don't let them see."

I understood humiliation. I knew how it could flatten you, how it could make you want to lock yourself in an attic and not come out again until everyone who ever knew you had forgotten about your existence. Oh yes, I knew all about humiliation. I knew a lot less about fighting back. I couldn't think of any brave, clever retort to say to Mr. Wooly. I didn't even say, "No."

All I did was not move.

"MOVE!" Wooly screamed it in my ear so loud it hurt.

Something popped into my head at that moment. It was like Wooly's scream had shaken loose a thought that had been hiding in my brain, tucked beneath all the other thoughts:

I am a boulder. Boulders don't move.

Something in my expression must have changed then too. All of a sudden Wooly looked at me, really looked at me. He pushed his glasses up on his nose.

There was a noise from inside the locker room, a heavy clunking sound.

"Is that young man having a seizure?" he asked, his voice turning very teacherly all of a sudden. "Is that what's going on in there?"

I have to admit, this pulled me up short. Was that what it was? Did Mason have seizures? It was possible that Wooly was lying to me in order to get past me. On the other hand, it made sense. It would explain why Mason had run away from me so frantically in the hallway. I had once seen a person have a seizure on the street. It was horrible-looking. Her eyes rolled back in her head, and her legs and arms thrashed around. She drooled all over herself.

"Get out of my way!" Wooly screamed. The kids crowded up behind him now, ready to storm in the locker room and see the infamous Mason Ragg having a seizure.

I am a boulder. Boulders don't move.

For a moment I thought Mr. Wooly might try and shove me out of the way. He might even hit me—he certainly looked angry enough to. I braced myself for a blow. For a second my eyes glanced up at Sybil, who was still holding up her camera, capturing the whole scene and part of me thought, Yes, do it, Wooly. Hit me. Then everyone can see what a maniac you are on *The Universe According to Sybil*.

But though he was a maniac, he wasn't a total moron. He knew he couldn't touch me without getting tossed out of the school.

"Andre!" Mr. Wooly screamed without taking his eyes off of me.

"Yes?" Andre said. He was right behind Wooly.

"Go get security."

Security! Not the principal?! Security!

We had one security guard, a big guy with a bald head and perennial sweat marks under his armpits who sat by the front door and looked bored. He was going to love this. I wondered if, unlike Wooly, he had permission to use force against me.

Mr. Wooly stuck his face close to mine. I could smell old coffee on his breath and could see the tiny red veins on the creases of his nostrils, that's how close he was.

"If that kid is having a seizure in there," Wooly said, "and he injures himself, or *drops dead,* then it will be your fault, Birnbaum. You hear me?"

If he had known the truth about me and my parents, he couldn't have said anything more perfectly designed to tear my heart out.

I am a boulder. Boulders don't move.

I felt tears burning my eyes, and my throat was swelling and every muscle in my body was begging me to let it move, but I had promised Mason not to let them see, and I would not let them see. Jeremy was with him. If things got too bad, she would get help.

I am a boulder, I am a boulder, I will not move.

I felt a cold tap on my back. The locker room door had opened. Jeremy appeared by my side.

"It's over," she said.

"Over?" I couldn't wrap my mind around the words. They had come so close on the heels of Wooly's comment about Mason dying that I felt a rush of fear.

"The seizure is over," Jeremy explained quickly. "He's okay. He's just resting."

Wooly made his move then, pushing past me into the locker room. I let my body be pushed aside. It didn't matter anymore. As the cops like to say, "The show is over, folks. Nothing interesting to see here."

My mind let my body have its way. I slipped down to the floor and sat there with my knees up and my head on my knees, eyes closed. I felt overwhelmed with exhaustion. I wanted to be back in my bed, alone. I wanted to sleep for three days straight.

I felt a light brush against my left arm, and I opened one eye to see that Jeremy had crouched down beside me. We looked at each other for a moment without saying a word. It had all been so strangely similar to that night two years ago, only back then I had been blocking the door from Jeremy, not Wooly, and it had not ended with everyone being just fine.

"You did a good thing," Jeremy said. "That was really . . . you know, heroic."

I nodded. I didn't feel heroic. But maybe it's one of those overrated things.

15

I almost felt sorry for the security guard. He came rushing through the door, his underarm stains already creeping farther down his uniform than I had ever seen before, ready for a full-blown riot. But when he burst into the locker room, he was told that he wasn't needed after all. He still hung around for a few minutes in the hopes, I'm guessing, that some new riot would break out. No such luck. Mason's teacher's aide appeared and quickly ushered him out. She must have had some harsh words for Wooly because he came out of the locker right after, muttering angrily to himself. He walked right past us without even noticing me and Jeremy on the floor. The noon bell rang. Gym class was over.

Jeremy went back to her classroom (GWAB had slipped out of the lunchroom for The Blue and White Rebellion, since they had lunch right before we did), and I changed back into my clothes and headed out of the gym. It was almost as though nothing had happened. Almost. But on my way out of gym class, Andre Bertoni failed to thump me anywhere on my body and no one made any farting noises as I passed by. If someone less of a bully magnet than myself had defied Wooly the way I had just done, there probably would have been some hooting or some "You rock"-ing. But no one knew what to do in my case, so they didn't do anything. And you know what? That was fine by me.

The part that wasn't so fine by me was having lunch with Izzy. With all the stuff that had happened in the gym, I had completely forgotten about Izzy and my suspicions. I even forgot to check inside the I ♥ Puffins tote bag to see if the cookies were gone before I went into the lunchroom. Of course the second I saw Izzy's head towering above everyone else's, it all came back to me.

Still, I didn't feel like I could just go up to him and say, "Okay you creep, I know it was you who took my Oreos all along," because I didn't have any real proof. It was all circumstantial evidence, as they say. Instead, I decided to simply not sit with him. That was a statement in itself. Unfortunately, Izzy spotted me before I could find another seat and started waving like mad with this crazy big grin on his face.

And then he gave me the thumbs-up.

It's really hard to snub someone who is giving you the thumbs-up. Try it sometime and you'll see.

"I heard all about it, man," Izzy said when I reluctantly

approached the table and sat down. "The hallways were buzzing with the news." He held out his bear-paw-sized hand and I had to shake it. "You are truly a hero, dude." He lowered his head so that it was closer to mine. "But why'd you do it? People are saying you were protecting Mason Ragg. They said that he got scared of doing this race with you and he made a run for it back to the locker room and you wouldn't let Wooly get at him to drag him out. Why'd you do that, man? I thought Ragg was your number one archenemy."

"He's not my archenemy," I said.

No, that title belongs to *you*, I thought.

"He never stole my Oreos, you know," I said.

"Really?" Izzy made the phoniest surprised face I had ever seen in my life.

"No," I said coldly, staring back at him.

"Do you know who did?" Izzy asked.

"Let's just say I have my suspicions," I said.

Izzy lifted his upper lip like he smelled something bad. "Why are you acting like that?" he asked me.

"Like what?"

"I don't know. Like a detective on one of those cheesy old TV shows."

That made me turn red in the face, which annoyed me to no end, since he was the one who should be embarrassed.

"I found my lunch sack in the boys' bathroom today," I

blurted out. "It was hung up on a piece of wire that was so high off the ground only a really tall person could have reached it."

Not very subtle, I know. But I was upset.

I watched Izzy's face go through some interesting changes. It was such a big face that all the little twitches were magnified—his eyebrows dipped down, his nostrils pushed out, his lips spread into a grimace, then contracted into a pucker.

"So you think I put it up there?" he said finally.

Faced with accusing him directly, I hedged a little bit. "Well, I certainly think it's a possibility."

"Okay," he said. "I did."

I felt a surge of dismay. There was a little piece of me that was hoping I was totally wrong.

"But," he added quickly, "that doesn't mean that I'm the thief."

My dismay moved directly to self-righteous anger. "Oh no? You *knew* I was upset about the whole Oreo thing! You *knew* I was trying to catch Mason in the act! If you saw my lunch sack and you *didn't* steal it, why on earth wouldn't you just give it back to me? Why would you hang it up in the bathroom?"

"I didn't steal it," he said. "I wanted you to find it. But I didn't steal it."

I grabbed my lunch and stood up.

It would have been a pretty dramatic moment. I was just about to call him a liar and find another table to sit at, but one of the hall monitors came into the lunchroom and told me that I was to report to the principal's office ASAP.

I guess I shouldn't have been surprised, but I was. Surprised and mortified. I had never in my life been sent to the principal's office. I didn't even know what a principal's office looked like.

Mason was already sitting in a chair outside the office when I arrived.

"Ms. DeRosa will be with you shortly," the secretary told me.

"Hey," I said to Mason, sitting next to him.

"Hey."

I felt weirdly awkward with him suddenly. I now knew more about him than I was sure he wanted me to know. I started to ask him if he was okay, but I had a feeling he might not like that, so instead I asked, "Are we in trouble?"

He shrugged. "Hard to tell."

"Hmm." I said.

There was a squirmish silence during which I heard Wooly's booming voice on the other side of the door, talking to the principal.

"I wasn't running away because of the race thing, you know," Mason said.

"I know."

"I mean, I didn't run away, *then* have a seizure. I ran away because I knew the seizure was coming."

"I figured," I said.

"Ok," he said. There was another silence.

"How did you know it was coming?" I suddenly wondered out loud, then wished I hadn't.

Still he answered me and didn't seem offended.

"I hear a train," he said.

"Really?"

"It's nothing weird," he said quickly. "It's my aura. A lot of people with seizures get auras right before they seize. Some of them see lights or hear music. Mine's a train."

"So when you get the hall pass and leave the classroom," I said, "it's because you're hearing the train?"

He nodded. "There's usually enough time for me to find my aide before I start seizing. I heard the train when those girls walked in the gym today, but I kept ignoring it, hoping it would go away. That was stupid. I waited too long." He paused, then tapped the evil genius side of his face. "Got *this* from waiting too long."

"How?" I asked, and once again instantly could have kicked myself for asking.

Still, I was really, really curious.

"I was taking a shower," he said. "I heard the train, but I thought I had time. When I started seizing, my hand hit the cold water tap and turned it off. This side of my face got a full blast of boiling hot water the whole time I seized. Burned it bad."

"Oh."

It was not quite like an M-80 firecracker being thrown at you in revenge for strangling a girl with her Molly Wildchild necklace.

"Can I ask you something else?" I said. I thought I was probably pushing my luck but everything was turned upside down and inside out today.

"Maybe," he said cagily.

"Do you really carry a switchblade in your sock?" I asked.

To my surprise, he instantly lifted his left foot and placed it on his chair. Then he hiked up his pant leg. I could see the narrow, oblong outline under his sock. He reached in and pulled out something metal and shiny and tossed it to me. I didn't catch it. I never catch things that are tossed to me. It bounced off my hands and landed in my lap. I looked at it. I'd never seen a switchblade in person, but I had seen them in the movies, and this looked like a bona fide switchblade. I didn't think it was in my best interest to be sitting outside the principal's office with a switchblade on my lap.

"Very nice," I said, picking it up by the corner and holding it out for him. I was sorry I'd asked about it.

"Don't you want to open it?" he said, not taking it.

"No. Nope. Here you go." I glanced up at the principal's door, expecting her to appear at any minute.

"Look," Mason said, leaning across to me. "There's a button on the side. Press it." Now I could hear some scraping inside Ms. DeRosa's office, like they were getting up from their chairs.

"Could you just—" My voice was rising with panic. They were going to open the door any second. "Put this thing away, will you!" I dropped it in Mason's lap. He picked it up calmly and held it in his palm. With his index finger he pressed a button on the side of the box.

Snick!

I flinched backward. Then I looked down. A tiny metal drawer had shot out of the side of the box, and inside it were three keys on a ring.

"My house keys," he said.

"Oh." There was a thin sheen of sweat on my face.

"I keep them in my sock because they tend to fall out of my pockets."

"Gotcha," I said.

He smiled. It was the evil genius smile. I hadn't imagined it. It was straight out of the comics, it really was.

The principal's door opened and Mr. Wooly stepped out. He glared at us. I don't think things had gone very well for him in Ms. DeRosa's office. She didn't look too happy either when she called me in.

"So," Ms. DeRosa said after I sat down in a chair on the opposite side of her desk. "Let's hear your version." She sipped at a metal thermos of coffee as she listened to my side of the story. I tried to be as truthful as possible. I was slightly less than truthful about Jeremy and GWAB. Actually I didn't mention them at all.

She listened really well. Not many people know how to do that. When I was finished, she gave me a short lecture about endangering a classmate with a serious medical condition and said she would be speaking to my sister as well (of course, Wooly would have told her about The Blue and

White Rebellion). Then she said she hoped she'd never have to see me in her office again.

I said, "I hope not too," and then wondered if that sounded rude, so I said, "Nice chatting with you." But that sounded like I didn't take this thing very seriously, so I bowed. Just like she was the Queen of England.

I told you I do idiotic things when I'm nervous.

Do you know what Ms. DeRosa did? She bowed back. Not just a dip-your-head bow either. She put down her thermos, stood up, and bowed deeply to me. I thought that was really classy of her. I like to think that each of us felt the other one deserved a bow.

But maybe she was just being polite.

16

After school, Jeremy wasn't waiting for me by the corner. I stood around for a while, hoping she'd show, but she didn't. I thought things between us might have improved because of what happened today. Obviously, I was wrong.

It wasn't until I was almost home that I remembered I had Penny Marshall's birthday in my pocket. I stuck my hand in my pocket and touched the paper, although I didn't really have to look at it again. The date was fixed in my brain: October 15, 1943. Now all I had to do was go through the October 2006 issue of *Retro TV Magazine* to see what time that *Brady Bunch* episode had been aired and I could pinpoint the exact timing for the surveillance camera. I might have to do a little more scavenging for a bigger dish so that I could bring in the signal more consistently, but all in all, things were looking good.

A calmness came over me. All the puzzle pieces were in place—or nearly. In nine days, if all went well, I was going to see the face of the person who had slammed a wrecking ball into my life. In a few days' time, his bad karma was going to come crashing down on his head like a grand piano.

Just then something occurred to me. I don't know why I hadn't thought of it before, but now that I did, I felt a shiver run along the back of my neck. Not only was I going to see the man's face, I was also going to see the whole crime. Everything. My parents' faces, the gun firing. My mother screaming and the gun firing again. Could I bear it?

You'll have to, I told myself. That's all is there is to it.

When I got home, Honey happily pounced on me as usual and I realized that lately my walks with her were pretty lame. Once around the block and home again so I could get back to work on Nemesis. Today I decided to walk her over to Riverside Park, where I could let her run around off the leash. She must have had a premonition, because she jumped around like mad when she saw me take out the Crap Catcher and she was already straining at the leash when we stepped off the elevator. She pulled the whole way to the park. When we got there, I took off the Crap Catcher and unclipped her leash from her collar. She shot off like a stretched-out rubber band that's suddenly been released. For a solid fifteen minutes she ran around me in a circle, her mouth stretched wide in that pit bull smile. When she finally winded herself she collapsed on the grass panting. I sat down with her, even though the ground was pretty cold. I watched the boats on the Hudson

River gliding past and a helicopter flying over the boats. I watched some little kids racing each other on the promenade. I didn't think about Nemesis or being fat or how Izzy had betrayed me. I was just . . . fine.

Honey probably feels like that all the time.

We sat there for a long time, and it was only when my butt began to feel a little numb from the cold that we started walking back home.

A half block away from my apartment, I saw a boy up ahead, holding something in front of him and having a hard time with it. He stopped every few seconds to rearrange the thing, lifting it higher, then dropping it down lower. It wasn't until I was a few feet away that I realized it was Arthur. Right after that, I realized that she must be holding the carton of *Retro TV Magazine*s.

"What's going on?" I asked, my eyes fixed on the box.

"I've been impeached," she said. She spat out the last word, her expression full of fury and disbelief. I felt like she wanted me to be shocked too.

"That's awful," I said. "Why are you taking the box back?"

I know that wasn't very tactful, but Arthur didn't seem to notice.

"Because it's *her* fault I was impeached," Arthur said, nodding contemptuously toward my building. "She steps all over my speech in gym class, and then she sneaks into the boys' locker room! She had no right to do that. We had everything all planned out and she hogged all the attention."

These were the most words I'd ever heard Arthur use at one time.

"I don't think she did it deliberately," I said as Arthur heaved the box up again. Part of me wanted to snatch it away from her and make a mad dash for the apartment. But I controlled myself.

"Yes, she did! She always has to be the boss. Well, now she is. GWAB called an emergency meeting after school and they took a vote. I'm out, she's in. She's the new president. Long live the queen."

"King," I said.

"Whatever. Anyway, I'm done with GWAB and I'm done with Jeremy Birnbaum." She shifted the box to her right hip and started to walk away.

"Wait!" I said. "I still have another week to look at the *Retro TV Magazines*."

Arthur didn't stop walking. "So?" she called back.

I hurried to catch up with her. "So this isn't fair. I gave you my clothes. We made a deal."

"I'm not breaking it," she said as she kept walking.

"Yes you are!" I must admit I was screeching now. "You've got the box right in your hands!"

"Not the box of *Retro TV Magazines*," she said.

"Well . . . well." Okay, now I was sputtering, this was so ridiculous. "What else are they?"

"The videos that Jeremy borrowed."

"Liar!"

There. I had completed the moment of drama that had been so rudely interrupted in the lunchroom today. I did it without thinking, and I hadn't really meant to be so harsh, but I tell you, I had had it up to here with being lied to that day (my hand is hovering about a foot above my head at the moment).

To Arthur's credit, she didn't get all huffy about being called a liar. She did the sensible thing. She put the box down, took off the lid, and let me look inside.

The thing was filled with videos. The spine of each video sleeve was labeled with a white sticker with neat black printing on it. Among them were *Charlie's Angels/Pom Pom Angels/October 14, 2006* and *The Brady Bunch/Katchoo/October 15, 2006*.

For several moments I was so confused that I didn't say a word. Finally, I managed to utter, "When did Jeremy borrow these?"

"This past Monday."

The same day the supposed old signals came through Nemesis.

"But . . . why would she do that?" I said this out loud to myself.

Now Arthur did get huffy. "Because they're great shows, why else?"

Yeah. Why else?

"Thanks, Arthur," I said, replacing the lid on the box, picking it up, and handing it back to her.

"I'll be by to pick up the *Retro TV Magazine*s a week from Saturday," she said.

I nodded, but I wasn't really listening. I was thinking hard.

Jeremy was in her room. When I knocked, she called back, "I'm busy!" I came in anyway.

She was sitting in her rocking chair, rocking back and forth. She stopped abruptly when she saw me and frowned. "I said I was busy."

"You look it," I said dryly. I folded my arms across my chest and stared at her.

"What?" she said, not meeting my eye. She started rocking again.

"I don't need to ask you *how* you did it," I said. "That part is obvious. You took that signal splitter I found at the Seventy-fifth Street demo site and you fed Arthur's videos into my TV. To get the image all fuzzy, you messed with the video tracking."

There was some satisfaction in seeing the surprised look on her face. Actually, it was very satisfying, since I had been such a complete sucker for the past few days.

"What I'd like to know is why you would do that to me," I said. I was so angry that my voice cracked. I'll tell you the truth, I was so angry I wanted to hit her.

"Did you want to make me look like an idiot, is that why?" I said.

She shook her head but didn't say anything and didn't look at me, she just kept rocking.

"Stop rocking!" I screamed at her.

She did, and now she looked up at me. With her hair all short like that, she looked older. Smarter. More serious. It was like she had been tricking me about everything, even her personality.

"WHY?" I yelled at her so loudly that I made her jump a little.

"Because . . ." she said, "because . . . because I felt sorry for you."

I think that was probably the worst thing she could have said. I turned around and walked right out of her room. Honey had been sitting outside the door, and I pushed her aside with my foot. I walked into my room, slammed the door, and furiously shoved my bed against it to keep it closed, since there was no lock on it.

Then I began to tear Nemesis apart. I ripped out wires, yanked apart cables. I took all my anger out on the thing. It now seemed like a useless, silly toy. I couldn't believe that I had ever thought it would work. I had been so *stupid!* And there's me, crowing to Jeremy about getting the signal, there's me, getting all excited about finding out Penny Marshall's stupid birthday, there's idiotic me, telling Nima all about my ingenious invention.

"Owen?" Jeremy was outside, twisting the knob and pushing against the door.

I took the green paper that said SLOB on it out from under the amplifier and put it back under my drawer. I took the satellite dish off the tripod.

"Let me in, Owen!"

I wouldn't, but she threw all her weight against the door again and again until it opened just enough to let her slip through. She stood there for a minute, looking around. I think she was stunned. Nemesis was in ruins all over my floor and I was sitting in the middle of it. A fat Buddha surrounded by garbage.

"Oh, I forgot to congratulate you," I said bitterly. "President of GWAB. That's sensational. You should be really proud of yourself."

"I'm not their president," she said. "I'm not even a member anymore."

"Yeah, right," I said. "That's why you chopped off all your hair."

"I did that for you," she said.

"For *me?*" I was so outraged that I swallowed a glob of spit and choked a little. "When did I ever tell you to chop off your hair?!"

"You didn't, but it was for you anyway." She sat down heavily in a clear spot of rug, hugged her knees to her chest, and put her forehead down on her knees for a moment. Then she lifted her head suddenly. "Didn't you ever wonder how I was able to become a GWAB member and not cut my hair?"

"Yes," I said. I had wondered about it, but not very hard.

"It's part of the initiation, you know," she said. "Everyone has to do it. But I wouldn't. They were going to kick me out, but Arthur said that maybe they could find something else for me to do. So they had a meeting and they came up with an idea. I had to steal your lunch from the lunch closet for two weeks straight. That was mean. I know it was, Owen, and I told them it was, but they said it had to be something that I wouldn't want to do or else it wouldn't count. I talked them down to just stealing your cookies."

My mouth fell open, just like they always describe in books, but it really did. "You stole them? *You* did? Not Izzy?"

"Izzy? Why would Izzy steal your cookies? And anyway, I thought you thought it was Mason Ragg."

"I did," I muttered, thinking about poor Izzy, trying to remember what I had said to him at lunch and wincing when I did.

"Look," she said, "it wasn't supposed to turn out the way it did. I even tried to get the cookies back to you. That first day I left them on the table you and Izzy usually sit at, but of course that day you didn't and Mason did and then, oh, it just all became this huge mess. I felt awful about the whole thing, and I just wanted to make it up to you."

"And making me think Nemesis was working when

it wasn't was supposed to make it up to me?" I said incredulously.

"It made you happy," she said.

"Well, yeah. Maybe temporarily. But come on, Jeremy, didn't you realize I was going to find out sooner or later that it was all a prank?"

"You said yourself that picking up signals was a long shot. When you hooked up the deli's surveillance camera's receiver to Nemesis and nothing happened, you wouldn't have thought someone was playing a prank with the old Freakout shows. You just would have figured that you just couldn't pick up those particular signals, right?"

It was so logical that I had a sudden urge to throw a satellite dish at her.

"Aren't you smart," I said glumly. "So how did you figure out how to bypass the Jaws of Anguish?"

"I didn't," she said. "It snapped shut when I put my hand in. But, you know . . ." she held up her arm and smiled. "Skinny wrists. I slipped right out. Then I set it again. It was a good trap, though. If it *had* been Mason, it would have got him for sure."

I know she was mostly just trying to make me feel better, but it did.

"Did you eat the facial hair bleach?" I asked, pretending to be upset. I really was hoping that she'd had just a tiny taste.

"Facial hair bleach? Eww, no! Did you put facial hair bleach in the cookies?"

"One time."

She thought for a minute and then said, "Maybe that was the time Izzy caught me."

"Izzy knew?"

"Well, I was at the lunch closet and I had your lunch sack in my hands and was about to get the cookies out when I heard someone coming. So I ran away, but I was still holding the lunch sack. I ditched it in the boys' bathroom. When I turned around, there was Izzy. He'd seen everything. I made him swear not to tell you. He was really upset. He told me all about Mason Ragg and how you thought it was him and how he carried a buck knife—"

"Switchblade," I corrected.

"Really? I thought it was a buck knife."

"Switchblade. And it isn't really a switchblade, it's a key holder."

"Oh. Weird. Anyway, Izzy said I was going to get you killed, and I promised him I'd fix it all if he just didn't say a single word to you about it."

"He kept his promise," I said.

Jeremy smiled. "I figured he would. He's a really decent guy. Anyway, that's when I wrote the note about following Mason. I knew that if you followed him, you'd see he wasn't the one stealing the Oreos and you'd stop trying to catch him, and that might prevent a hideous buck knife attack. Switchblade attack. Whatever. But see"—she rubbed her hand across her cropped hair—"it was all for nothing. I cut it anyway. Well, the GWAB members cut it, actually. They passed the scissors around and all took a few snips. I wanted to punch them the whole time. But I just couldn't do it anymore, sneaking around and lying and seeing you get all excited about Nemesis. It felt too crappy. And anyway"— she eyed me cautiously—"Mom's gone. It's not like she's going to care."

I looked at the sad little red cap of hair, with a hank of it tufted up at the top.

"Dad would have said you looked like a pumpkin," I said.

"Ha-ha," she said dryly. Then she said. "Probably"

"And Mom would have tracked down every member of GWAB and made them sorry they ever learned how to use a pair of scissors," I said.

"Yeah, she would have. Mom was tough." Jeremy lifted her eyebrows and smiled. She looked around at the bits and pieces of Nemesis and her smile disappeared. "Maybe we could put it back together. We don't have to give up yet."

I nodded.

"You know," she said, "I always thought there was a chance Nemesis really could work. I thought if anyone could do it, you could."

"Thanks, Jeremy."

"I'm not Jeremy anymore, remember."

"Oh, right. I kind of got used to you as Jeremy."

"Yeah, me too. Maybe I'll hang on to it for a while longer."

17

There's this thing called The Three-Month Rule. It works, it really does. The rule is that it takes three months for things to really change.

For example, it takes three months to:

1. Go from 57 percent fatter than the national average to only 10 percent fatter than the national average
2. Grow out a bad haircut
3. Realize that your radio telescope doesn't work and turn it into something entirely different
4. Become pretty good friends with someone you had previously thought was a psychopath
5. Have people stop making fart noises when you walk by them

There are some things that can happen more quickly than three months. One of them is to patch up a misunderstanding between friends. Well, with some people it might take three months, but Izzy happens to be one of those forgive-and-forget types. He did sulk a little when I sat down with him at lunch the day after I had accused him of being a thief.

"Oh, so now I'm your friend again?" he said.

"Jeremy confessed," I said. "She told me that she was the one who was taking my Oreos. I'm sorry, Izzy. I'm sorry I called you a thief or thought anything rotten about you."

"Oh, man," He raked his hands through his hair. "Did you tell her that I didn't snitch on her? Oh man, she probably hates me."

"She knows you didn't snitch," I assured him.

He blew out a puff of air that sounded like a pneumatic bus door opening up. Then he remembered me and opened up his huge paws in a pleading way. "I was between a rock and a hard place, man."

"Understood."

"You sure?"

"I'm sure. But let me ask you this. How long have you had a crush on my sister?" I said.

"What?" He narrowed his eyes at me.

"It doesn't take a genius to figure it out," I told him.

He blushed, then shot me a shy look. "A while, I guess. Does she still like that Andre dude?"

"Andre's not worth one of your hangnails, Izzy. Jeremy is no dope. She'll figure that out."

Which brings me to the last item on my list . . .
It takes three months for a girl to:

6. Really appreciate a guy like Izzy and figure out that a guy like Andre is not worth one of Izzy's hangnails

So three months later takes us right into January. It's one of those January thaws in New York City where the temperature creeps up to over forty degrees and you actually see a few people walking around in khaki shorts. Everyone heads to Central Park to squeeze in a little Rollerblading or bike riding or . . .

Okay, I can't take it anymore. I'm trying to set the scene for you and make this very literary, but really there is something I'm dying to show you. I'm going to skip over all the literary stuff, if you don't mind. I'll just let you know that Mom and I went shopping at Macy's and bought some new clothes for me. I had stuck to a diet, and although it was torture at first, it became easier as the weeks went on. Now I was swimming in my old clothes. That's not the thing I'm dying to show you, but I thought you should know that. Jeremy was out at the ice-skating rink with Izzy. Good luck renting a pair of skates in size 13, I thought, but he'd squeeze into a size 10 just to get a chance to flop all over the ice with Jeremy by his side. They're just friends, good friends, but I wouldn't be sorry if they dated one day. You know, when Jeremy was eighteen or so.

After Mom and I went shopping, I told her there was something I wanted to show her. We took the bus back uptown and got off by the Museum of Natural History. In January it's not usually all that crowded outside the museum, but it was today. Good weather and all. There was a big crowd gathered off to the left side of the steps and that was where I led Mom now.

"What?" she said, smiling at me. "What is it?"

"Just wait," I said.

Some of the people in the crowd were clearly in a line formation, but others were standing around watching something. We joined them. I grabbed Mom's hand and inched us through the crowd to get a better look.

The momo cart was festooned with its usual flags, and Nima was smiling his usual good-natured pirate smile. What wasn't usual was a loud clicking-tonk-tonk-slapping noise. Nima saw me almost right away. His smile spread even wider, and he waved me over. I pulled Mom with me.

"This man here, my friend Owen Birnbaum," Nima announced to the crowd as he put his arm around me, "this the man that built *she*!"

His arms spread wide toward the contraption that was clicking-tonk-tonk-slapping on his cart.

My satellite dish was now a momo Ferris wheel, painted with a bright yellow sun in the center and red and blue rays coming off the sun, like the design on the Tibetan flag (Jeremy had helped me with the painting part). Around its edges I had attached little metal brackets that served as tiny seats for momos. As fast as Nima could make the momos, a pivoting metal arm made of scrap pipe with a pair of food tongs soldered to the end snapped them up and placed them on the Ferris wheel, which spun slowly, turned by a bicycle chain and a washing machine motor attached to the back. The little momos traveled up, up, up. Then as they started their downward ride, the little bracket seats made a fast flipping motion. The momos flew into the air, one after another, like tiny circus performers, and landed in Nima's large steam pot.

Do you know what the crowd did? They applauded.

It wasn't the Nobel Prize, but it was still pretty nice.

Mom applauded too, after looking a little stunned. Nima gave us a heaping plate of momos and we sat down on the steps of the museum.

"Owen, you're a genius," she said.

"Not quite. I'm one point short."

It was one of those perfect days. I love those days. But they also make me nervous because I know that lurking behind every perfect day are a few less-than-perfect bits and pieces. One of those pieces was underneath my desk drawer. I hadn't known what to do with it after I destroyed Nemesis. I couldn't throw it away, yet I couldn't look at it either.

But because today was a perfect day, I opened the drawer up and took out the little green paper with SLOB written on it.

When people die, all the things they've ever touched or have ever belonged to them should be buried with them. Like the Egyptians used to do. It doesn't seem fair that a person's writing should still exist on this planet while the actual person is gone.

SLOB

It was the last thing my mother ever wrote. In a perfect world, the last thing your mother ever wrote would be something like, *My darling son, I love you more than I can ever say. I'll always watch over you.*

But my mother worked in a deli. The last thing she wrote was an order she took from a customer. The customer who killed her.

SLOB

Our deli's shorthand for salami on an onion bagel.

All of a sudden I knew what to do. I put the piece of paper in my back pocket and yanked on my coat and hat.

"Going out," I called to Mom.

"Where?" she called back, but I was already out the door. I took the stairs because I didn't want to wait for the elevator. And anyway, I needed to move. I had too much energy chasing around in my body.

I walked down to Broadway, then West End Avenue and past the school, which lately didn't seem quite as menacing as it once had. Mr. Wooly still hated me, but he mostly ignored me. I'm guessing he didn't want to be called back into the principal's office anytime soon.

I entered Riverside Park. It was loaded with people soaking up the sun that was seeping through the cold air. I headed straight for the promenade. There were few boats on the water and there were icy patches here and there, but the water was moving slowly. I took the slip of green paper out of my pocket. A gust of wind made it flap wildly in my hand, but I held on to it.

I said a prayer. I've never prayed before, so I don't know if I did it right. I prayed that the police would one day catch the man who killed my parents. But in case that didn't happen, I prayed that karma would kick in. I prayed that the murderer would be the unluckiest man who ever lived. That he'd always be losing his wallet, missing the bus when it's raining, pulling out his back, getting pelted by snowballs, or stepping in dog poop. I prayed that he would feel like crud five days out of the week and have intestinal gas pains for the other two days.

I know that's not exactly compassionate.

But for now, it's the best I can do.

I folded the paper in quarters, ripped it in half, then again, and dropped it in the Hudson River. The pieces bobbed around for a moment, like they didn't know what to do, until they were finally carried off by the wake of a passing tugboat.

At the last minute, I sent off one more prayer. That the man who murdered my parents has someone in his life who thinks he's a better person than he actually is.

Ok. That really is the best I can do.